THE CYBORG'S IDENTITY

BOOK 5

Benoit Lanteigne

80 Mapleton Rd, Unit 11-80
Moncton, New-Brunswick, Canada
E1C 7W8

Benoit Lanteigne

80 Mapleton Rd, Unit 11-80
Moncton, New-Brunswick, Canada
E1C 7W8

https://thecyborgscrusade.com

Book Layout © 2016 BookDesignTemplates.com
Edited by Eliza Dee
Book Cover Design by 100 Covers

The Cyborg's Crusade / Benoit Lanteigne. -- 1st ed.
ISBN 978-1-7387526-3-8

AVAILABLE NOW IN THIS SERIES

The Cyborg's Crusade

The Cyborg's Warning

The Cyborg's Riddle

The Cyborg's Fortune

The Cyborg's Identity

AVAILABLE FOR PREORDER

The Cyborg's Attack

CONTENTS

Do you want a free short story that serves as a prequel to The Cyborg's Crusade? Then, join my newsletter on my website https://thecyborgscrusade.com.

Brothers

Chapter 1

Valar 5, 2134, on the Nirnivian calendar

Entered room. Diabo recognized Janice, grinned. Gestured me to get closer camera; obeyed. Heh, too late turn back.
—Thoughts of Wrathchild, Hocmar 28, 2134, on the Nirnivian calendar

"Won't ya lookit that, Wrathchild's givin' me a gift! Such a pretty thing. She's a real prize, ain't she?" As he smiled, Diabo caressed Janice's hair with his fingers. The touch possessed a surprising amount of tenderness. "I could have so much fun with her." The red hand on Janice's face brought a shiver out of Melissa even if she realized Diabo only meant to get under Daniel Ricdeau's skin.

"Don't you touch her!" On the screen, the Commander shook his fist while blood flushed to his cheeks. "I'll kill you with my bare fists even if it's the last thing I'll ever do!"

"Oh?" The crimson beast laughed. "I'd like to see ya try!" Then he dismissed the notion with a wave. "Relax, I ain't gonna do anything. I'm not that kinda guy, more of a romantic. Freaking nice hostage, though." Diabo gestured toward his goons. "Tie her up with the rest of 'em and wake her up. Torture ain't no fun when there's no screams."

Looked at Rose on screen. Distressed. Chewed nails. Worried for sister... Felt bad. Owed her everything. Betrayed her.

Used to trust me, now hated me. Deserved it. Still needed her to understand.

—Thoughts of Wrathchild, Hocmar 28, 2134, on the Nirnivian calendar

Filled with hesitation, Wrathchild risked a few steps closer to the monitor, though she only dared stare at the floor. "Rose; sorry," she whispered as she forced herself to lift her head and gaze into the holy one's eyes.

Despite the low volume, Rose heard her and so did Diabo. The boss grimaced but remained silent. Rose, however, rested her palms on her hips and yelled, "Don't you dare! Don't you dare apologize! I'm not falling for it. You've shown me your true colors a long time ago!"

"Allison! Janice tried kill Allison! Had to stop her. You love Allison too!"

"Shut up!" Rose interrupted while her glower intensified. "I don't care about your excuses. Wrathchild, you're dead to me."

Never called me Wrathchild before. Always Melissa. From her, worst insult. Lost all faith in me. Didn't deserve forgiveness. Still wanted it. Knew wouldn't happen.

—Thoughts of Wrathchild, Hocmar 28, 2134, on the Nirnivian calendar

Chapter 2

Brucie couldn't believe they'd dragged Janice into this, literally. With a gasp, he closed his eyes for a few seconds. Then he opened them, hoping her capture ended up being an illusion brought by his hyperactive imagination. Instead, he glimpsed the BBR goons tying her to a bench. Once more he blinked, praying against the odds that when his eyelids rose, the scene would have changed by some miracle. It did, but not in a pleasant way. Now the thugs waved smelling salts under her nose.

Encouraged by the powerful odor, Janice groaned and twitched. She lifted her head, shook it. After a few seconds, her muscles tensed up, and she straightened. Though Brucie couldn't see her expression, he assumed she realized what had happened. He grimaced as his eyes watered. For years, he had trained, learned to fight. Through that time and effort, he had grown huge and strong, all to protect himself and others from bullies. And what had been the point? Brucie had failed to stop his brother from capturing him. He couldn't save James. Even the woman he loved he couldn't help. So much work and he remained defenseless when it mattered. The thought sickened him. How, he had no idea, but Brucie swore he'd rescue everyone stuck in this goddamn church.

As Brucie attempted to form a plan, visions from the past distracted him. He tried to concentrate, but to no avail. Images of him loitering near the Ricdeaus' pool filled his mind. In those days, Janice had despised him, considered him a young horny brat slobbering over an older woman's body. That was correct. Back then, Brucie hadn't understood how special she was, and he wouldn't have had they not bonded over daddy issues. That connection had led to a date at a fancy restaurant, where they had indulged in a copious meal and blue paradise cocktails. Eventually, they had made love, Brucie's first time. Oh, he hadn't been a virgin, far from it. In fact, he had enjoyed a ton of sex during his school years, but he'd never cared for his partner on an emotional level until then. Too bad he'd returned to his old patterns. Memories of that fast-food joint flooded his brain. How that cute redhead had sat on his lap. How Janice had stormed inside with such a furious glare that a scared kid had dropped a cup of juice. How he had pleaded for an open relationship. How Janice had dumped his ass. That had been the greatest mistake of his life, worse even than attending this cursed funeral, and he hadn't managed to fix it. Perhaps if he had listened to Pierre.

Pierre had always liked Janice and approved of them dating. The elder sibling believed she served as a good influence. And, given his own experiences, Pierre didn't care about the age difference. When he'd learned of the breakup, he had been almost as devastated as Brucie. However, while Brucie had concealed his sorrow out of machoism, Pierre had displayed it in full view.

***

A few days after the breakup, Pierre invited Brucie for lunch, claiming they needed to talk. In dismay, once they arrived, Brucie recognized the establishment where Janice had caught him cheating. Though his heart sank, he kept a strong facade, unwilling to let his sadness through. While

Brucie wished to run away from this place, he followed Pierre inside. In there, he felt as if everyone stared at him, shaming him for his disgraceful behavior. The urge to flee he fought back and endured while Pierre ordered two servings of mishusq chips.

This being a fast-food joint, they received their meals within five minutes and sat at an isolated table in a corner. Seconds after, loud crunches echoed as Pierre munched his snack. As for Brucie, he didn't touch it. Pierre frowned and pointed at the filled paper plate. "Are ya down, Brucie? Ya ain't eating much lately."

"Down?" Brucie forced a laugh. "Nah, feeling great, bro!"

"It's Janice, ain't it?"

"What? Come on, dude"—he aimed his thumb toward his own torso—"this piece of male hotness ain't gonna cry for no chick, ya know." With a self-satisfied smirk, Brucie leaned back in his chair and linked his hands behind his skull. "I can get a ton o' babes, easy. And younger too. My dick's never been this busy, bro."

Pierre scoffed before shaking his head. "Brucie, you're not fooling anyone. You like that woman. A lot. And she's good for ya." Pierre adopted a perceptive smile. "Maybe it ain't too late, 'cause she freaking likes ya too, but it ain't gonna be easy. Crawl back to her on all fours and tell her you're a major asshole. Swear that you ain't gonna do anything that dumb again."

"Nah—nah, man, no way. Yeah, I like her, but I want an open relationship, ya know. I can't deprive the ladies o' my awesomeness!"

"Ah!" Sarcasm tainted Pierre's tone. "Always thinking 'bout your junk, eh, Brucie? Too bad. Janice, she's a nice woman. Believe me: I've dated enough monsters to know the value of a nice woman." Pierre had a reputation of being unlucky in matters of love. While he was a master of seduction, his conquests only brought him grief. Like Cheryl, who had stolen his truck, or Judith, who'd trashed his stuff as a punishment for an affair he hadn't had. "She got a great personality, a great body. Plus, her family's loaded. Hey, I ain't saying you should marry her 'cause o' that, but"—he winked—"it's a bonus. Why not give exclusivity a shot? What do ya have to lose?"

"No way, dude. Brucie Garland ain't ever gonna settle fo' one chick. Would be a waste o' my talent, ya know."

Pierre frowned. "Do ya think you're being strong?"

"Huh?"

"'Cause you ain't. You're a freaking coward." He waggled a lecturing finger. "Yeah, you can punch a guy, and lift weights, but that ain't real strength, Brucie. Facing your feelings, admitting you were wrong and fixing it. That's what being strong is about. So why don't ya stop acting like a scared kid and go to her while you still have a chance?"

Brucie gritted his teeth as his eyes watered and he slapped the table, resulting in a loud bang. Several people stared at them, including the staff, but he didn't care. "What for, huh? So I can screw her over like Dad did to Mom?"

With that, he sobbed and a vision from the past popped into his mind. One that had never left him; it lingered in the shadows. His mother had been speaking on the phone with a friend, unaware little Brucie played with blocks under the table. A month ago, his father had disappeared. The family had fallen into complete disarray, and his mom had taken the brunt of it. "No, no, Hilda, don't... No, listen, they're all freaking bastards. Men, they're total jerks. All of 'em. Don't fall for his crap, he ain't worth it. Lookit what Hank did to me. I shouldn't have got married, biggest mistake o' my life. He's gonna do the same to ya. Issat what you want, Hilda? He hit you once, he ain't gonna stop." Those words stuck with Brucie. Now an adult, he understood his mother hadn't meant it. She was trying to help someone out of a toxic relationship and vented about her own frustration. If she had been aware of Brucie's presence, she would've expressed herself differently. But she hadn't. Brucie had heard everything and didn't forget.

Pierre rubbed his chin. "So, lemme get this straight. You're 'fraid you're gonna treat Janice like crap, so to avoid that, you treated her like crap." A sigh escaped his lips. "That's what 'em geniuses call a self-fulfilling prophecy, Brucie."

"Whatever, I had 'nough o' this shit. I'm outta here." Brucie stood and took a few steps away.

"Hey, bro!" As he yelled, Pierre jumped to his feet so fast his chair fell on its side, accompanied by a bang. "We ain't our dad. We can make our own choices, and our own mistakes. Yeah, if ya get back with Janice, you gonna mess up and hurt her. And she's gonna do the same to ya. That's just how it is, and it sucks, but"—Pierre exhaled—"when it's with the right person, the bullshit's worth it. Don't let her get away, or you'll regret it fo' the rest o' your life." He paused and whimpered. "Janice, she's your Ramona."

Brucie rolled his eyes. The infamous Ramona, Pierre's so-called soulmate. His big brother had fallen hard for her, claimed they shared the purest love. But then again, if Ramona had cared so much about Pierre, why had she abandoned him like their father had?

"Whatever, dude. Whatever."

***

In hindsight, Brucie wished he'd listened. He gazed toward Janice, so close yet so far away. If only he hadn't been so stupid. Pride and fear had motivated his decision. Now she didn't trust him, and with good reason. And how did he react? With dumb pranks and innuendo, as if it was a joke. Well, no more. For once, he'd be strong and face his feelings. Somehow, he'd earn Janice's trust again, no matter the cost.

Chapter 3

Wrathchild's interruption angered Rose far more than it should have. That traitor didn't deserve any sentiment—not even hatred. Yet she failed to control her emotions. Long ago, Rose had believed in her, despite Wrathchild's horrendous actions during her youth. Rose had assumed a life of abuse had caused the rashness. But Wrathchild had spat on that faith, betraying her and Nirnivia.

Rose's fury distracted her from her other woes, but with Wrathchild stilling her tongue, fear and anguish replaced the rage. Unfortunately, she preferred the anger. From the start, this had been a nightmare. That James and Brucie faced peril had tormented Rose to begin with, and now her dearest sister had joined the hostages. The thought of losing Janice proved unbearable. That their relationship had deteriorated made it so much worse. Rose hoped they'd reconcile someday, but if Janice died, then it wouldn't happen, finishing the relationship on a sour note.

Three of the people Rose held closest to her heart might not survive. How had it come to this? She glanced toward her father. Thanks to his Zarg complexion, the stress rendered his skin tone paler than her own anemic shade. The old man appeared almost white as snow. Though Rose supposed that was natural given Janice was his daughter. As she watched Daniel's pained and teary eyes, a realization struck Rose: Plague wasn't worth this suffering.

"Dad," Rose said in her sweetest voice. "Please, stop this. It's going too far. Let's return Plague."

"Hey, missy!" the Koporal shouted before Daniel could reply. "Remember your promise? I do, and I've had enough." Tigh jabbed his thumb at the door. "Get out."

Daniel lifted an open palm toward Ron. "That won't be necessary, I'll handle her." Then he offered Rose a warm smile. That reminded her of when, as a kid, she had been well-meaning but misguided. "Princess, we can't give in to terrorists. I know it's hard, but you have to be strong."

"Brucie, James and now Janice are there—not to mention the other hostages. They're strangers, but they have families and friends who care. Are you telling me they must die today so NISDA can keep Plague? Is he worth that much? I don't think so."

Daniel grimaced. "It's not so simple, princess."

"But..." A frown formed on Rose's brow and she crossed her arms. "How can you say that when Janice is—"

"Janice is a soldier. She read the job description. In this situation, I'd sacrifice anyone, including her. Janice knew that when she signed up, and she'd want to be treated like everyone else. A Commander can't have personal feelings affect his judgment."

"That's so cold."

Daniel opened his mouth to counter, but his lips quivered without a sound. Then he indulged in a deep inhale and tried again. "It's not like it's easy. I'm devastated. All this time, I've been trying to figure out a way to rescue Janice. It's not looking good. I wish I could release Plague, but that's not an option."

While she considered the argument, Rose shut her eyes and rubbed her brow. Daniel's reasoning possessed logic, and she understood his point. Yet a horrifying truth revealed itself, contorting her face. "You'd do it for me! If I was out there, you would give Diabo anything he wants!"

"Princess—"

"Janice is your daughter!"

"So are you."

Rose shook her head. "No, I'm a kid who lived in your house! Janice is your biological daughter, your flesh and blood! Doesn't that count for something? Why can't you save her? Why can you save me?" As if struck by a blow, her father recoiled. No response came; Daniel just stood there breathless. Rose had hurt him and regretted it, but propelled by rage, she couldn't stop. "Why?" she continued in tears. "Answer me! Tell me why!" But Rose already knew. That was the worst part. Daniel loved Janice with every fiber of his being and would do anything for her, but his sense of duty refused to let him. That Daniel would have caved had it been Rose was obvious. He made it clear with his embarrassed silence. The reason? The beautiful yet cursed wings attached to her body. It wasn't Janice's fault she was born wingless. Driven by anger and sorrow, Rose almost brought up those facts and more, but Ron jumped between her and Daniel.

"Hey, cut the guilt trip, missy. That's low even for you. I'm disappointed. With all those freaking speeches about morals I expect better out of you. Yeah, he'd save you, same for me. Trust me, it ain't because I like you. You're a special case: the Melkar. Oh, but I'm not telling you anything new, huh? So, stop this madness and apologize or I'll kick your holy ass out of here with my own foot." Tigh paused for a second. "You think this is bad? It's nothing compared to what would happen if we gave in to BBR's demands. Do you want people to think we bow down to terrorists?"

With a hard swallow, Rose realized the Koporal spoke the truth. Daniel was a good man who'd raised her like his own child. No, he didn't deserve blame. That should be reserved for the actual villain, Diabo. "I'm..." Her voice trembled, and she had difficulty looking at him. "I'm sorry, Dad." A smile appeared on his face and she expected he'd accept her apology, but before he said anything, words shouted by Brucie echoed through the chamber.

Chapter 4

In Brucie's mind, a plan began to form. Okay, that might have been an overstatement. It was more like the shadow of an idea, and a desperate one at that. Still better than nothing, though. The memories he had relived served as the key. Against the odds, the past images he had endured brought hope along with pain. Or did they? He supposed he'd find out.

Brucie gazed at Janice, who proved as helpless as him. From his seat, only the back of her head remained visible. How he wanted to rescue her from this mess. Maybe his "plan" was pure foolishness born out of his desire to be the hero who saves the girl. Perhaps it was an irrational hope that if he succeeded, he'd win her heart.

Those doubts in mind, Brucie studied the other prisoners. A varied group of people surrounded him: men and women, young and old, the single trait they shared being their vulnerability. Suddenly, rescuing those lives seemed like an unfeasible dream, yet wasn't it worth a shot?

On the screen, the Commander, his Koporal and Rose argued about their next step. The botched assassination attempt rendered the possibility of a peaceful resolution nil. Daniel would never give in to terrorism, Ron even less so. A bloodbath remained the lone option. That was why Brucie had to take care of the situation. He stared at Diabo and swallowed hard. The decision made, Brucie then focused on James. The human trembled while breathing at a rapid pace.

"Hey, dude," Brucie murmured, "don't ya worry; I'll get us outta here."

"Um, don't do anything stupid."

Brucie nodded and turned his attention toward his sibling. He understood what he had to do, but it caused an emotional toll. His heart rate increased and sweat covered his brow. This had to succeed. Sure, Diabo had morphed into a horrible brute, but for certain, a bit of Pierre Garland existed in there somewhere. Brucie sighed; no sense in delaying further.

"Hey, bro!" he shouted. "This ain't like ya! I guess Doctor Death also made ya a freaking coward."

"Brother!" The crimson beast adopted a disturbing grin. "Ya been a quiet boy so far. Too bad it didn't last."

"Seriously, dude, hiding your sorry red ass behind hostages? Why are ya so damn scared? Shameful."

Crossing his arms, Diabo growled. "Brucie, I ain't gonna break your neck 'cause I need you, but don't push me."

"The Pierre Garland I knew was a fighter, ya know? He didn't hide; he kicked butt! How 'bout we settle this like men? No more wussy stuff, just balls-out action."

"Oh, this is gonna be so freaking lame." The monster sighed and then shook his head. "Whatever, I gotta hear this. Whatcha got?"

"Simple, dude: we fight. A boxing match, like the old days, ya know? You win and ya get Plague. I win, ya surrender."

Demented laughter from Diabo and his thugs filled the room. Meanwhile, the hostages gasped in disbelief. James yelled, "What the hell?" Or rather Brucie deduced it was him, since no one else would utter that expression. The skepticism he understood. Diabo possessed strength beyond any Gorumar. A physical competition was doomed to failure, so Brucie's proposition equaled suicide.

A smirk appeared on Diabo's lips. "Heh, I figured it'd be stupid, but come on! A boxing match? Ah! Your head ain't right. Ya never beat me before; no way you can now. Got a death wish?"

Brucie scoffed. "Afraid I'm gonna crush your winning streak, huh?"

"Yeah, sure." Diabo chuckled. "I'll admit, it sounds kinda fun. I'd even stick to my end o' the bargain. But, here's the problem: you ain't in charge. You running your mouth don't mean shit."

"Right. Let's fix that." Brucie stared at the monitor. "Commander Ricdeau, sir?"

"Yes."

"How 'bout ya agree? Trust me, I can do this."

***

In the war room, everyone fell silent. None could believe their ears, least of all Rose. No question, her bodyguard had cracked under the pressure. He wouldn't make such a ludicrous offer otherwise.

"Okay, I didn't expect that." Tigh frowned and scratched his head. "What do you think, Dan?"

After a sigh, Daniel lowered his neck and rubbed his chin. Then he gestured at an officer, who pushed what Rose assumed to be the mute button. "The boy has a plan. It sounds insane, but at this point I'm willing to try anything."

The shock of those words left Rose reeling, but she soon recuperated and advanced toward her father while pointing an incredulous index finger. "Dad, you can't be serious! He'll get himself killed! There's no way he can win, and even if he did, we can't trust Diabo. He won't release the hostages."

"Son of a gun, missy's right for once." The Koporal's lips twitched. "Brucie's lost it."

Daniel shook his head. "No, he hasn't. Look at his posture; his expression."

"I ain't seeing anything special."

"Well, my eyes are better. This isn't how a man who's lost his mind looks. The line of his jaw, the way he's positioning his fists. No, this isn't desperation, it's all wrong. Brucie's quite confident. More than I'd expect. And he's not stupid, he knows he can't win." After a short pause, Daniel snapped his fingers. "Oh, and he's not suicidal either, in case you were wondering."

Rose gulped. Could Daniel really be considering this? "But, Dad, don't forget Diabo is his brother. It's obvious Brucie is devastated!"

"Oh yes, he's stressed—I won't deny that. But he's faring better than you give him credit for. Brucie's tough, and he's smart enough to realize this can't be solved with a boxing match. He has something up his sleeve. I have no idea what it is, but Brucie's confident it can work. At worst he'll buy some time." Daniel groaned. "Princess, I got nothing. If you have a suggestion, I'll listen." The room hushed. Rose had none, and neither did the military officers. "No? Well, then, I don't have any choice. Unmute the channel."

"Yes, sir!"

Again, Daniel faced the monitor. "Diabo, beat Brucie and we'll release Plague and the others! You have my word."

The red monster burst into laughter. "Your word? Ah! After the shit ya pulled, that ain't worth jack! This is dumb as freak, but I'm feeling kinda nostalgic... fine, I wanna do this."

Brothers

Chapter 5

Right away, BBR goons cleared up the area where the priest performed the ceremonies, the biggest part being removing the altar. Two previous blows from Diabo had shattered the holy furniture anyway; it needed to be replaced. Soon, the so-called ring was ready. No rope, nor mattress to cushion falls. No gloves either. They'd fight with bare fists. A first for Brucie, but he heard claims that the glove worsened the risk of brain damage and only reduced chances of superficial bruises and cuts, so that might have been for the best. At any rate, this would be an unusual battle.

Before long, thugs approached Brucie's pew and untied him. An urge to grab their throats and squeezed the life out of them filled him, but he resisted. That would get him killed. He needed to focus and save everyone. Without a sound, Brucie followed the terrorists as they led the way. Three steps separated the spectator seats from their pretend arena, and Brucie now climbed them. They served as one of the borders for the "ring." Better be careful, lest he forget about them while trading blows and trip in a fatal fall. Once up there, Brucie swallowed hard. The space ended up tighter than he'd hoped; this was a narrow spot. Plus, the shape proved strange, more of a triangle than the classic rectangle. Ah well, it would have to do.

Pierre stood on the left side cross-armed, so Brucie went for the right. With every step, his legs weakened as doubts entered his heart. Could this succeed? He had to be insane. Perhaps searching for a sign that Pierre still existed in that monstrous shell he had become, Brucie gazed into Diabo's eyes. The crimson beast stared back, yellow irises bursting with coldness. If any compassion for his younger brother remained, Diabo failed to show it. With a wince, Brucie lowered his neck and closed his eyes. The glower drained the determination out of him. No, this couldn't work. Not now that Pierre had turned into Diabo. And yet... was that the truth? For all his cruelty, Diabo remembered their past together. What was a Gorumar if not the sum of their memories? That thought in mind, Brucie gave a quick glance toward Janice for courage and took a deep breath. Then he straightened and glared at Diabo, unflinching, unwavering. Brucie's resolve elicited a mere scoff out of his sibling.

Now that Brucie had overcome his doubts over battling Pierre, he noticed the woman standing between them, holding a small Korono bell used during weddings. Brucie deduced she intended to use it to signal the end of a round. A slight smile formed on Brucie's lips as he wondered how Rose would feel about such a usage of a sacred object. It wasn't as if they had many alternatives, he supposed. Besides, a more pressing question posed itself: would this referee be neutral? As Diabo's goon, she might attempt tricks like speeding up or slowing down her ten count. Brucie debated raising an objection but declined to. What did it matter? A standard victory would be impossible.

Still, Diabo pointed at her and said, "Hey, don't ya try any funny business, ya hear me? Ya better be fair or I ain't gonna be happy 'bout it." He shrugged and refocused on Brucie. "Caught ya lookin' at her, figured what ya worried 'bout. That's good 'nough for ya?"

"Yeah, sure." Brucie bobbed his head toward the other BBR thugs littering the area. "Except if one o' them shoots me in the back o' something."

A genuine laugh escaped Diabo. "Fair 'nough!" His voice grew louder. "Boys, if any o' ya interfere, I'll rip your spine out. There ya go, bro!"

"Thanks."

Silence returned and Brucie studied Pierre's body. He'd almost tripled in girth and his height had increased. Those arms possessed incredible reach. Beyond that, the way he'd destroyed the altar showed his already considerable strength had also gotten a boost. As for speed, it was impossible to tell for certain, though the extra mass might have slowed Diabo down. In short, prospects were dire.

When the referee signaled the start of the match, Brucie exhaled in relief. Any longer and he might've lost his nerve. Both men danced around each other, keeping their distance. Contrary to his normal brashness, Diabo declined to attack. Instead, he moved his fist in a manner taunting Brucie to do so. If that was what he wished... Brucie attempted a feint with his left. Against the odds, Diabo blocked the jolt that never came. That caused an opening in his defense and Brucie threw a full-forced punch into his stomach. Upon impact, Brucie gritted his teeth and recoiled. A sob echoed as he retracted his arm. That hurt like a freaking bitch. With a rapid breath, Brucie nudged his fingers to ensure he hadn't broken any and Diabo burst into a chortle.

"Told ya it's a bad idea."

"Ain't gonna give up, bro."

"Heh, it's your funeral."

Brucie smirked. "Nah, it's Dad's."

A roll of the eyes came from Pierre. "Always a wiseass, huh, Brucie? Gotta teach ya a lesson. Take this!"

The vocal cue served as a warning, but even without it, the blow posed little threat because of its subpar speed.

Brucie ducked, and it flew above his head. Next, Diabo struck from the side, but Brucie hopped backward. The dodge succeeded, but his feet landed on the edge of the stairs. Brucie wavered and extended his arms to regain his balance. Somehow, his brother didn't capitalize on his mistake and the dance continued. Every strike fired by Diabo missed the mark. Thank God for the lowered swiftness. Meanwhile, Brucie connected three more times. Two in the face, which was as solid as the guts, and another in the ribs. Pierre displayed no reaction and Brucie doubted he suffered any pain.

After that last hit, the referee rang the bell. Round one over. Obedient, Brucie returned to his "corner" and Pierre did the same. There, a BBR thug wiped the sweat off his brow and offered a sip of water, which Brucie accepted. Dehydration wouldn't help. Meanwhile, he studied his bruised knuckles. The attacks he'd landed had caused more damage to him than Pierre. That might be an issue. Could his armored body be harmed?

As Brucie pondered that question, the goons bandaged his injured fingers and the second round began. It started much like the previous one, though more aggressive. Diabo attempted pummeling Brucie from the start, but his sluggishness rendered the effort nil. As they traded blows, images from their days in Pierre's makeshift gym flooded Brucie. Him knocking Pierre down for the first time. Pierre congratulating him on a battle almost won. Both of them sharing a well-earned beverage. Those thoughts choked Brucie with nostalgia. A few errors occurred because of this, but nothing that allowed Pierre to smack him. Did the same memories assault him? Based on Diabo's watering eyes and grimace, it seemed to be the case. At least, Brucie hoped so.

Despite the similarities with his past experiences, there was one important distinction: they'd never boxed in front of a crowd. Caught up in the excitement, the BBR brutes screamed encouragements for Diabo and jeered his opponent. The prisoners remained silent at first, but eventually they joined in. The spectators' cheers gave Brucie a rush. In different circumstances, this could have been a grand occasion. As he told himself that, Diabo fired a devastating uppercut, but Brucie dodged sideways. The assault left the red monster's defense open and Brucie punched him four times in a row, wincing with each impact.

Diabo grinned. "Brother! Ya got better!"

"Yeah, well, I trained hard, ya know."

"Good! I'm proud o' you."

That sounded like the old Pierre. Brucie's scheme might succeed. His opponent outclassed him, but everyone has a weakness. This battle saddened Brucie because of their history, and he prayed his sibling endured the same torment. Deep inside, Diabo was still Pierre Garland. He had to be. Pierre had been a decent man who loved Brucie and would never harm him. Boxing like this should remind Pierre of their previous bouts and the moments they shared. Ultimately, he'd realize this could only end with Brucie injured or dead and he'd surrender. Brucie suspected the plan would appear far-fetched and foolish to anyone else, but they failed to grasp the significance of the sport for him and Pierre. As he stared into the yellow eyes, his confidence grew. Earlier they'd glowed with hatred, but concern had replaced the animosity. A sense of hope emerged from within Brucie, and as he indulged in it, Pierre threw a powerful jab. With a gasp, Brucie rolled out of the way at the last second. Propelled by the strength of his punch, Diabo slipped down the stairs. Crashes echoed as he tumbled on the floor below. Mouth gaping, he blinked twice, and the referee began counting. Diabo shook his head, regained his composure. When he understood what had happened, he hopped to his feet at the count of five.

While gritting his teeth, Diabo glowered at Brucie and mimicked slashing his throat with his index finger. Uh-oh. That was a bad sign. With a hard swallow, Brucie raised his defense. In a flash, Pierre climbed up again. Though Brucie expected it, the hook proved so fast he couldn't react. Pierre's fist connected with his face, and he flew backward, landing on his belly. Brucie spat out a tooth, then another. Blood dripped from his nose and lips. He attempted to get up. The world spun around him as his head ached and he collapsed again. A single punch might have finished him. After a deep breath, he struggled once more. Somehow, he stood up on seven, ears ringing and on the verge of throwing up. Thank God the referee rang the bell.

Back in his corner, goons wiped off Brucie's blood as he reeled. The savage strike had even affected his eye, and his field of vision grew narrower. That bastard Pierre had faked his lack of speed. On the positive side, that suggested he'd rather not harm Brucie, so he pretended to be slow and missed on purpose. That gave credence to Brucie's plan, but the fall down the stairs had angered his brother, and in his rage he'd attacked with his full velocity. Would he keep that going for the following round, or would he revert to his merciful ways? Another blow implied defeat, so Brucie prayed for the latter.

Filled with apprehension, Brucie started the third round. Pierre ended up choosing both options. The crimson beast struck faster than before, yet not quite at his maximum. That made evading challenging, but it remained possible.

Except Brucie couldn't counter anymore. The flurry of punches proved so intense, dodging demanded his full concentration. The one-sided dance went on and on. Then Diabo tried another hook and swung so hard he left himself wide open. Without thinking, Brucie aimed a jab. It landed on Diabo's nose and a few red droplets dripped out of the nostril. Blood! He'd drawn blood. No chance to gloat, for Diabo's fist collided with his stomach. Brucie's mouth gaped as his insides threatened to slide up his throat. Before that happened, a powerful uppercut reached his chin, and he fell, spitting out another tooth. The referee began counting. While wailing in pain, Brucie rolled and attempted to get on all fours. That failed in a bout of coughing. Blood escaped his gullet and stained the floor. What torture... he yearned to lie on the ground forever. And why not? There was no way he'd recover. Then he remembered why he was doing this. With a wail, he lifted his neck and glimpsed poor anxious Janice. Brucie frowned. Don't ask him how, but he got up on the count of nine.

Diabo shook his head. "Should've stayed down, brother!"

"Come on, dude! One lousy punch ain't gonna finish me, I ain't so weak!"

"Fine!" He smirked. "I'm having fun anyway."

And so the waltz continued. Brucie found himself at a disadvantage. The fierce pain dampened his concentration and his swiftness. That was a problem. He needed his dodge; he couldn't block such assaults. Somehow, he still avoided Diabo without trouble. Pierre displayed mercy. He knew Brucie stood on his last leg and thus gave him a chance: the improbable plan was working! Pierre didn't want to hurt his little brother...

Then a spectator yelled an insult at Diabo, who glowered at him. Deep down, Brucie realized he shouldn't exploit Pierre's distraction lest he unleash his fury once more, but his instinct got the best of him. He pummeled the beast in the guts, his own bones cracking under the impact. To stop the beating, Diabo struck him in the shoulder, dislocating it. Brucie's arm dangled as he landed on the floor. Now, it was over for real. Forcing a hard swallow, he closed his eyes and let himself drift toward sleep. That was when these words echoed: "Please, don't get up, brother."

That changed everything. He couldn't give up. Not when he was so close. Brucie mustered his strength and somehow got on his feet with only one arm. A groan escaped Diabo, and he threw a jab, but it lacked force. It served as a small push rather than a real punch, but that was enough to send Brucie back to the ground. While he coughed like a madman, he rose again at the count of nine.

Pierre shook his head. "You're screwed! Ain't got a prayer. Give up, brother." That almost sounded as if he begged.

"No! Never! Ya wanna end it? Ya gotta KO me!"

"Brucie, stop!" a woman's voice yelled. Janice. Brucie's heart warmed as he realized how much she worried for his safety.

"Sorry, Janice, I gotta do this."

"No, don't!" Janice's volume increased even more. "Stay down, please! You were freaking awesome, but you're done!"

Too late. He stood up again, though he wobbled. Diabo slapped his forehead. "Ya goddamn idiot. I know what you're doing. Ya figured I'll get all fuzzy inside. Then I'll see the errors o' my ways and let the hostages go. Shit, maybe we'll be a happy family again. That's a fairy tale, dumbass. It ain't how it works in real life. For a minute, I thought you'd try something clever. You disappoint me. How many times I gotta say this? I ain't Pierre Garland no more. I ain't your brother. You mean nothin' to me. Give up."

"No!" Brucie roared. "I can still fight!" How he managed his next feat, he had no idea, but he leaped toward Pierre and grabbed him by the throat with his functioning hand. Unfazed, Diabo tossed him on the floor without breaking a sweat.

"Got a death wish, bro? I'm 'bout to grant it..."

"Yeah, maybe I do!" Brucie murmured as he rose. "I ain't a quitter! Quitters are freaking losers. You're the one who taught me that! So I ain't gonna give up. Ya can knock me down a million times; I'll get up again and again! If ya wanna end it, ya'll have to kill me! Ya talk big, but can ya really do it?"

Diabo chortled. "What's that? Ya think I give a crap 'bout ya? Brucie, you idiot." He gritted his teeth. "I hate your guts, always have! Dad left, and I got stuck with you. You screwed me. Without ya, I'd have been better off. I could've finished school, made sumthing outta me. But nah, gotta take care of lil' bro." He scoffed. "Wanna know why I agreed to box with ya? 'Cause I wanted to punch the shit outta ya and ya gave me an excuse to."

"Oh yeah? I don't believe you! If that's true, prove it! Come on! Kill me! Just do it! I dare ya!"

Perhaps in shock, Diabo recoiled. Though he attempted a glare, he ended up shivering. Then he rubbed his brow, took a deep breath. Once he exhaled, he frowned and dashed toward Brucie, fist in the air. Brucie braced himself for impact, yet he doubted it would come. Sweat covered his face, but he still believed in Pierre. Diabo wound back his punch. His knuckles came an inch from Brucie's cheek but continued past it. Instead, the arm wrapped itself around Brucie, then the other did the same, hugging him. Both of them breathed heavily without a word, until Pierre whispered, "I told ya, I ain't your brother no more!"

With that, his hand grabbed Brucie's neck and an intense pressure pushed him backward. A loud crack resounded, accompanied by shrieks of terror. Again, Janice yelled his name. Brucie wondered why he saw the ceiling. Then he understood. As he closed his eyes, he yearned to laugh at the cruel joke of it all, but his broken body refused to do so.

***

Around Diabo, people gasped and screamed as he crushed Brucie's spine. Even his own goons shrank back in shock. Wrathchild's mouth gaped until she covered it with her fingers. Soon, she fell on her knees and retched. As for Diabo, he attempted to turn away on the off chance someone spotted his eyes watering. That ended up being difficult thanks to the crowd's size, so he walked toward the door to the room where the priests prepared for the coming ceremonies. About midway, Diabo peeked at Brucie's broken cadaver and his lips twitched. Then he averted his gaze and kept going. He'd had to do it. That realization had come when he'd grasped how much he cared for his brother still. The thought of hurting Brucie had almost resulted in him giving up, which implied surrendering to NISDA. With Plague, Wrathchild, and Diabo captured, it'd be over for BBR. For years, he'd claimed stopping Doctor Death was the most important thing in the world. That mission he'd deemed sacred. Yet, today, he'd considered abandoning it. And so, he'd had to kill Brucie. Prove to himself nothing would ever prevent him from reaching his goal. Now he felt assured that was the case, for he'd surmounted the hardest challenge possible and remained unwavering.

Chapter 6

In the war room, Rose and everyone else witnessed the gruesome murder. She screamed Brucie's name at the top of her lungs, but he never heard her. By then he had become a lifeless cadaver, torn to pieces. Sickened by the view, Rose turned her head. How could Diabo have committed such a heinous act? Yes, he'd often proved ruthless, but Brucie...

Part of Rose yearned to fall to the floor and cry until she drowned in her tears, but she had work to do. The passing of her bodyguard and friend strengthened her resolve. There would be no more death. She would make sure of that.

"Dad, we have to talk." Though her voice was weak and strained, the confidence in it grew with every word. "This has gone too far. We have to return Diabo's men—Plague included." Daniel didn't reply. Instead, he glanced at her with a saddened expression. Perhaps Daniel experienced guilt since he'd played a part in the tragedy.

"Now wait a goddamn minute, missy." The Koporal sprang forward. "What about not interfering, huh? I'm getting you out of here." On that note, Ron reached for her. Without delay, she struck him in that special way Brucie had shown her years ago: in the middle of the throat. Despite the blow's softness, it cut respiration, so Tigh recoiled and coughed. Rose hated using such a cheap move against him, but she lacked alternatives.

"Dad, please, this is futile." Rose sighed. "We can't win. Brucie died today because of our stubbornness. Are we supposed to lose everyone else? For what? A dying prisoner who won't cooperate no matter what?"

"We can't give in to freaking terrorists!" Ron repeated as he gasped for air. As far as Rose was concerned, he'd uttered that tired line more than enough.

"Well, I for one don't see why we must abandon all those people. I don't see why my big sister should sacrifice her life just so Plague can mock us from his cell. Dad, will you be able to look into Mom's eyes and explain why her daughter died today when you could have saved her? You already lost your son."

Daniel turned his head, but not fast enough to hide the grimace forming on his lips. "Janice is a soldier. Your mother will understand." Regardless of his effort, the retort sounded fake.

"We still have options." Ron raised his index finger. "Our troops are ready. We can storm the church."

"Really?" Rose groaned. "That'd be a bloodbath! Allison would use her power and the hostages would be caught in the crossfire. Any survivors Diabo would then execute to make a point. Is that your wish, Koporal Tigh?"

Before Ron answered, the Commander said, "Princess, Ulgorack knows I want Janice back, but... what you suggest goes against everything I believe in."

"Dad, what choice do we have? Brucie died for nothing. Please don't let Janice, James and the others suffer the same fate. I told you not to let Brucie fight. If you'd listened, he would still be alive. Don't make the same mistake twice!"

Daniel remained silent and cast his gaze downward in shame. Regret filled Rose. He didn't deserve that reprimand. It wasn't his fault; she had spoken out of desperation.

"Don't you blame him!" The Koporal's cheeks reddened as he glowered at Rose. "We didn't stick a gun to Brucie's head. It was his stupid idea." Rose ignored him. That bastard wouldn't yield, so she might as well focus on her father. Though Daniel yearned to follow her advice, his sense of duty stopped him. He feared it would be a fatal error in the long run. Maybe so, but Rose's heart assured her otherwise.

Another argument entered Rose's mind, the irrefutable kind. However, the notion gave her shivers. Would she truly dare? What a despicable act she pondered. She almost rejected the idea, but then the image of Wrathchild carrying Janice popped into her brain. Next came James and the joyful moments they'd shared. Brucie's braveness followed. Sometimes, you have to bend your principles. Rose swallowed hard.

"I... I didn't want to say anything because it's complicated, but I had a vision earlier. I may be wrong, but I think Ulgorack told me to save everyone, no matter what."

Eyes widening, Tigh aimed at her with an accusing finger. His jaw contorted in anger. "You lie! You can't fool me. Dan! She's lying, don't you realize that?"

Daniel rubbed his chin without responding. After a second or two, he mumbled to himself along with a slight nod. The Commander stared toward the screen and Rose did the same. The picture vanished. Diabo ended the transmission. "Contact Diabo, we'll exchange Plague for the hostages."

"What?" an incredulous Ron shouted. Overwhelmed with relief, Rose exhaled, then hugged her father. His arms embraced her back. In the distance, Nicky typed on her keyboard, carrying out the task. The Koporal took a step toward her. "Belay that order!" After that, he stared at

Daniel and whispered, "Sorry, old friend." His tone grew louder, not to mention stricter. "It seems his daughter's capture has impaired our leader's judgment. Mr. Daniel Ricdeau, as second officer, I am now relieving you of command for the duration of this mission." A groan escaped Tigh, and he gestured to a few nearby soldiers. "Escort Mr. Ricdeau and Her Holiness out of here. Make sure they don't interfere."

As she rested her hands on her hips, Rose gritted her teeth. "You bastard!" she shrieked. Ron shrugged off the insult. The three privates approached at a slow pace while glancing at each other. Given the circumstances, the Koporal was justified. Rose understood they had to comply, but no doubt apprehending both the Commander and the Melkar terrified them.

"Don't be too hasty, sons." Daniel offered a paternal smile. "My judgment isn't compromised. I believe this is the best course of action, and not because of Janice, or Her Holiness's vision."

The men hesitated.

"Come on, that's bullcrap!"

"Is it? Remember, Ron, Jade Carlson is in that church and the Council asked us to prioritize her rescue. That's reason enough to release Plague." The Koporal winced. "If you assume command, Ron, a committee will review your decision, and chances are they'll agree with me. Then you'll be disciplined. You know the Council will back me up."

"Yeah, I guess so." Tigh frowned. "But I have to do what I think is right for Nirnivia." Again, he gestured to the soldiers, but they still wavered. "Don't be idiots. Disobey, and I'll court-martial your asses. Do it, and I'm the only one responsible."

That was enough encouragement for the soldiers, and they advanced toward Rose and Daniel.

"Please, Mr. Tigh!" In tears, Rose dropped to her knees and joined her hands as if in prayer. "It's not too late, don't do this."

"Your Holiness"—Ron averted his gaze and scratched behind his head—"this isn't personal. Your dad's my best friend; I've known you all your life. I've always felt like I'm your grumpy old uncle or some crap like that... sorry, this is my duty."

The privates dragged them away. It was over. Rose had run out of options. The Koporal wouldn't listen to her. Despite their defeat, Daniel adopted a serene expression and accepted his fate. How Rose envied his calm. Panic filled her. That idiot Ron would storm the church. They'd lose not only the hostages but a great number of soldiers. Allison would make sure of that. And for what? James, Janice and so many more would be murdered, suffering the same fate as Brucie. God knew Rose had tried. Sometimes, you give it your all and still fail. She cursed herself for failing on this day. Soon, they reached the door, and it opened.

"Hey, you guys! Answer me already? Hello! Don't pretend you're not there, I see you!"

That voice... that sensual feminine voice. Daniel gasped and Rose joined him. Both recognized that woman. How could it be? They faced the monitor and there stood Janice, waving.

***

Wrathchild told me to stay hidden, but I didn't listen. Curiosity got the better of me, so I crawled out of my hole and watched Diabo fight Brucie while I prayed nobody spotted me. If only I'd followed her advice instead, then I wouldn't have seen what I saw. To this day, I still vividly recall how Diabo murdered his own brother in cold blood. I threw up in disgust. Thank God I didn't scream. Don't ask how I managed not to. After he dealt with Brucie, Diabo ended the communication and prepared to leave. I didn't understand why and didn't care. As far as I was concerned, it was good riddance. Except then he remembered about me. Diabo wanted to bring me along, but they couldn't find me. He became furious and swore like a sailor. Alarmed, I snuck under a bench and got lucky: BBR was in a hurry, so they left me behind. Once they were gone, I got out and untied a few hostages. Janice asked me to free her so she could contact the war room and explain what had happened. I did. Over there, they burst into celebration. Rose begged to see me; I obliged. She was so happy she cried tears of joy. That Diabo had left so suddenly worried Daniel, but not enough to crush his enthusiasm. They promised soldiers would pick us up soon. The hostages were all shaken, and so was I. Still, we made it. We went through hell and it was hard to believe it was over. Or that we'd lost Brucie forever.

—Thoughts of James Hunter, Hocmar 28, 2134, on the Nirnivian calendar

***

The nightmare had ended, and it had turned out better than expected. Or at least, that was what Rose's brain kept repeating. James, Janice and the remaining hostages had survived. What a relief. And yet her heart disagreed with her mind's assessment. Brucie's demise weighted upon her soul. That BBR had given up and left for no clear reason troubled her father, but Rose's exhaustion muted her own worries. She only cared about James and Janice's imminent return to the complex.

After Janice contacted them, her dad received an urgent communication. The old man had been speaking on the phone ever since, and he fumed. When the call finished, a frowning Daniel Ricdeau walked toward Ron Tigh, who stood beside Rose.

"Diabo may be dumb, but he tricked us!" The Koporal's nose wrinkled and Daniel added, "The hostages were a diversion like we thought. Plague's gone."

"What the freak? The place was on high alert. How did the bastard slip through?"

Daniel shrugged. "Stalker, of course. He infiltrated the prison and got Plague out." Rose's mouth gaped in shock. That Stalker had achieved such a feat despite the increased security showed his incredible skills. "We expected it and were prepared. Stalker was almost caught, but one of our own helped him: a guard named Hal Campbell."

"You mean that guy was a goddamn spy?"

"Seems that way, but Hal's been working for us for years." Both paused and considered the facts. Then Tigh frowned.

"Wait!" he said. "Why the freak did they take hostages? All that did is tip us off and put the prison on high alert."

After a groan, Daniel shrugged. "Really, I have no idea. At this point, I'm willing to settle for 'Diabo's just a big idiot.'"

"Heh, fair enough."

Rose watched in amazement. Minutes ago they'd nearly reached for each other's throats, and now they cooperated as if nothing had happened. Great friendship implied that kind of understanding, she supposed. Her dad realized Ron had acted like he had because he'd felt it was necessary. As for the Koporal, he trusted Daniel, and once the crisis was resolved, he relinquished command without complaints.

No need to talk or apologize. All was forgiven. Deep down, Rose wondered if she and Hunter would ever share such a profound bond. Would he display the same forgiveness should the situation demand it? Somehow, she doubted it.

At any rate, Rose wished she could have let it go as easily as Daniel. Tigh's behavior appalled her. The fool had endangered innocents, and for what? BBR had triumphed regardless. NISDA's efforts had been doomed from the start. Rose knew she shouldn't blame him and judged revenge a futile endeavor, but rage, fatigue and grief overwhelmed her and she failed to stop herself.

"Well, BBR won and we've lost a lot." A furtive glance she fired at Ron. None could deny the venom tainting her voice.

"Why not just come out and say what's on your mind, huh, missy?"

Rose rested her hands on her hips, the same posture that had killed her biological father. At that moment, part of her wished it would prove deadly once more. "You're an asshole, Tigh!" The various officers gulped. Vulgar language in public was rare for her, and it caused an impact. "Janice's two teammates, Brucie and several Nirnivians died for no reason! BBR won anyway! We should have surrendered Plague from the beginning. It wouldn't have changed anything. Didn't I tell you it was useless? But you didn't listen. You wanted a fight and were too proud to admit defeat, so you sacrificed all those lives needlessly."

"That's right, and I'd do it again!" She gasped and Ron smirked. "What, you think your way's better? We can't give in to freaking terrorists. It'd send the message that terrorism works. If we listened to you, it'd be much, much worse in the end! BBR and other organizations like them would pull more crap since they'd figure we'll cave in. Sometimes, good people die. Deal with it."

"Oh, you're so stubborn you won't admit when you're wrong. A real leader knows he shouldn't fight a battle he can't win and that it's better to retreat and live another day than perish."

The Koporal nodded. "Yeah, that's true. Let me guess, you're the one to make that call? What the freak do you know about military strategy, anyway? You crippled us with budget cuts. Why don't you stick with religion? Heh, you'd mess that up too." Rose sought an argument to counter his tirade but alas found none. With time, she would have figured something out, but Ron didn't give her a chance. "Besides, don't you dare get haughty with me." He pointed an accusing index finger toward her sternum. "Missy, you violated the Melkar's most sacred rule. Don't deny it: that vision was a goddamn lie."

That took the air out of Rose's lungs. With the commotion rising around her, she had forgotten her sin. Even with a million years of preparation, she could never refute Ron's claim. She'd lied hoping she'd save everyone. That horrible choice would haunt her for the rest of her existence. The Melkar served as a holy prophet, guiding her disciples toward the afterlife. To distort a vision or fake one was the vilest transgression the Voice of God could commit. Such an act might not only condemn her to nothingness but also the followers she deceived. Yes, Rose had had good intentions, but she'd committed an atrocity. Once, she'd heard an expression from earth: the road to hell is littered with good intentions. Though she possessed little knowledge of hell, and the exact meaning baffled her, she judged it fit the situation.

Ron groaned and shook his head. "You know what your problem is?" A touch of sadness lingered in his tone. "You can't make sacrifices. Sometimes, you have to make sacrifices. Yeah, it's difficult, but—" He sighed. "Ah, forget it. I'm tired and you won't listen to me anyway. You don't respect me. I wonder why I still have a shred of respect for you." The Koporal headed for the door, but then he turned his head and fired a final stare at her. "Oh, and about me being an asshole—yeah, I am. Assholes aren't popular, but they're needed. You use yours almost every day, don't you?" With that, he left. Daniel grinned at his friend's last remark. Looking at her father, Rose swallowed hard. Whether she wanted to or not, she had to confess.

"Dad"—Rose sobbed—"I... I'm so ashamed. You remember when I told you about the vision I had and Ron accused me of lying?" He nodded. Not surprising he remembered: the sham had persuaded him after all. Rose opened her mouth to continue but hesitated. That man idolized her and thus would be so disappointed. She struggled to find the words. "Ron was right. I'm sorry, Dad, it's unforgivable."

A sweet laugh escaped Daniel's lips. "Oh, princess, your father is old, but he's not senile yet." Then he patted her shoulder. "You twitched. Dear, you can be an amazing liar, but that one was too much for your talents."

Eyes open wide, Rose remained standing still for a second before she recuperated and said, "But... but you changed your mind because of that fake vision!"

"No, I didn't." Daniel's smile widened. "When you broke your most sacred rule, it made me think, and I reached the same conclusion as you. You did something horrible, but at least, princess, you did it for the right reasons, so I can forgive you."

"That seems too easy. That I had good intentions doesn't absolve my sin."

"No, but it's only natural for a parent to forgive his child no matter what."

Rose chuckled in a humorless manner. "Isn't the parent also supposed to punish the child?"

"Yes, but with you it's unnecessary." Daniel winked. "When you do something wrong, you punish yourself, so I can sit back and relax. Rose, you made a mistake; everybody does, even the Melkar. Ulgorack knows I've made my share." Daniel averted his gaze as he recalled a few past offenses. "Learn from it so you never repeat it. That's enough for me. It's been a long day; let's drop it for now, shall we?"

That sounded like a fine idea to Rose. She exhaled in relief while savoring Daniel's kindness, but then a troubling memory crept inside her, causing a shudder. "Dad, Brucie is dead. What am I going to do without him?"

"It's okay, we'll find another bodyguard."

She grimaced. "That's not what I meant!" A sob echoed, and soon after, tears rolled down her cheeks again. "Until Hunter arrived, Brucie was the closest thing to a friend I had, and he's gone. It won't ever be the same."

The instant Rose finished that sentence, Daniel hugged her. "I know, princess. Brucie might not have looked it at first glance, but he was a nice boy. We'll all miss him. It won't be easy, but you'll get through this."

Chapter 7

After escaped church, headed nearby hideout. NISDA tried stop us, but with Allison made it through. Stalker saved Plague. What Diabo said anyway. He hid true plan avoid leaks. I hoped Plague okay, but wouldn't believe was safe till saw him with own eyes.

—Thoughts of Wrathchild, Hocmar 28, 2134, on the Nirnivian calendar

Diabo, Wrathchild and the others arrived at the rendezvous point not long after they left Onel. There they at last reunited with their captured comrades. Screams of joys and victory echoed through the cave as their leader entered. Against the odds, they'd prevailed. Diabo high-fived Stalker. Melissa assumed he would have done the same for Plague, but ever since his wife and daughter had died, the decrepit mutant detested touching people. Despite the protective clothing he wore, Plague feared physical contact.

"Great job, Stalker!" The crimson monster grinned. "You're freaking awesome!"

"Thanks, boss."

"When I heard you took a church hostage to get me out, I figured you'd lost your mind." Plague chuckled. "You sure showed me. Thanks, Diabo."

"Ain't no need to thank me. We're a family. 'Sides, it's cause o' you! All I could think of was that stupid hostage thing, and then I asked myself, what would that smart son o' a bitch we call Plague do?"

Plague alive. While had doubts, Diabo's rashness paid off. Was happy Plague okay, but also sad. Rose hated me. Sure, knew already; still hurt be reminded. And Diabo killed brother. Gave me chills. Own little brother... merciless. Then noticed new guy. New guys always suspicious.

—Thoughts of Wrathchild, Hocmar 28, 2134, on the Nirnivian calendar

"Hey!" Diabo gestured toward the lone unfamiliar face. "Who the freak is he and why the shit is he wearing a NISDA uniform?"

Plague presented an open palm. "Relax, boss, that's Hal Campbell. No need to worry, he's with BBR now. He was one of my guards. He had a change of heart and helped us. Hal's trustworthy, I'll vouch for him."

"Yeah, he saved my ass back there." Stalker offered a thumbs-up to Hal. "Without him, I'd be rotting in a cell. I'll vouch for him too."

"Hmm..." Diabo rubbed his chin. "Ain't wanna be paranoid, but we gotta be careful. Tell me, why did ya betray NISDA?"

Hal stared into Diabo's yellow eyes. Impressive considering few could endure the beast's gaze. "Plague told me a story. It was convincing."

Diabo tapped his cheek with his index finger as he contemplated that claim. "Yeah, I know what you're talking 'bout. Plague can spin a tale. Ain't trusting you yet, kid, but I'll give ya a chance. You'll start low. Prove your loyalty and you'll rise soon 'nough."

"That's fine with me, sir. NISDA is the same."

***

Celebration over, found place be alone and thought what happened. Thought about Rose. How betrayed her. Wouldn't

be forgiven; not anymore. At least, did her favor. Deserved it. Was all could do. After while, Plague came talk.

> —Thoughts of Wrathchild, Hocmar 28, 2134, on the Nirnivian calendar

"Yo, Wrath, what's going on?"

Melissa shrugged. "Not much."

"Always a woman of few words, huh?" Plague chuckled. "Nice to see you again, kid."

"Nice see you too. Feared wouldn't."

Plague nodded. "Yeah, you and me both. I figured I'd die in that cell. Thanks for saving me." Wrathchild smiled; he almost sounded as if he'd expected they'd abandon him. There was no way: they stuck together, no matter what. "One piece of good news: Diabo agreed to lie low until Nirnivia calms down. I hope he learned his lesson. We can't fight both sides and win. About time he cooled his temper." Melissa acquiesced. The boss often went too far; that was a fact. "What's on your mind, Wrath? Don't say 'nothing.'"

No need lie. Plague knew how felt about Rose. All did. Stalker ignored it. Diabo hated it. Plague understood it.

> —Thoughts of Wrathchild, Hocmar 28, 2134, on the Nirnivian calendar

"Talked to Rose."

"Ah." Plague reached out to pat Melissa's shoulder but stopped himself before he touched her. "I take it that didn't go well?"

"Despise me. Said never forgive me."

"I wouldn't worry about it." Wrathchild aimed a curious look at him. "You betrayed her and Nirnivia, and she doesn't even know why. It's normal she's angry, but Her Holiness is forgiving by nature. You two will make peace yet."

"Doubt it."

"Heh, that's your call. Come on, this is a happy day, you can mope later."

Chapter 8

A military vehicle picked us up soon after and we left that cursed church behind. I swore I'd never return. The horrors that happened there tainted the beauty within forever. Janice didn't speak during the whole trip, maybe because she was in shock. Whatever the reason, the silence offered plenty of opportunity to remember Brucie. Even if I'd witnessed Diabo tear him apart, I couldn't believe Brucie was gone or that he wouldn't tell any of his stupid jokes or pull an asinine prank. I'd only known the guy for a few months and we hadn't started off on the right foot, but I missed him a lot... I'd never experienced death before. Both my grandpas died, but I was too young to understand. And I'd lost pets, but that's nothing compared to a human being... well, okay, so Brucie wasn't human either, but he sure was close enough to pass for one.

The void inside was so painful, I didn't dare imagine how I'd have felt if Brucie had been a childhood friend. Some people there had seen their parent, spouse, or kid coldly murdered, so I guess in a way I was lucky, but that didn't make it easier. Though the ride back was short, it seemed longer thanks to my dark mood. A "welcoming committee" waited for us: Rose, Daniel, Kristina, and a bunch of strangers. Rose was so relieved she nearly jumped on me. She held me so tight I couldn't breathe, but I didn't complain. The poor thing cried and kept repeating she feared I wouldn't survive. I can relate: for a while I doubted it too. Once done with me, Rose hugged her sister. Janice almost pushed her away.

Yeah, those two had issues all right. The reunion was pleasant, but there was obviously someone missing.

— Thoughts of James Hunter, Hocmar 28, 2134, on the Nirnivian calendar

"I'm glad you are alive and well," Rose said again, though her voice didn't reflect any joy. "It's silly, but I almost expected it was a hoax and that Brucie would be there mocking me."

"Um, I know." James scratched behind his head. "Uh, I was there in person and I still can't believe he... it's so unfair."

Daniel lowered his gaze. "Brucie was a good man and he'll be missed."

We exchanged comments like that for a few minutes. While it was useless, we couldn't stop. All part of the mourning process, I guess. Janice stayed quiet the whole time and cringed when we pronounced Brucie's name. That confused me, but it would become clear why.

— Thoughts of James Hunter, Hocmar 28, 2134, on the Nirnivian calendar

"Valardir won't be the same. Brucie was a spark of life around here."

Everyone nodded at that remark from Rose except for Janice, who clenched her fists and frowned. "Will you shut up about Brucie!" she yelled. "Some of us don't want to remember!"

Janice's anger dazed us. Brucie was her friend too, how could she be so cruel? Nobody realized how much his death weighed on her. Yes, it upset everyone, but Janice took it the worst.

— Thoughts of James Hunter, Hocmar 28, 2134, on the Nirnivian calendar

"Janice... yes, this is difficult, but talking helps us cope," Rose replied once the shock subsided. "Brucie's passing is painful, but that doesn't mean we should forget about him. Even sad memories have worth."

A fierce glare Janice aimed toward the alleged prophet. "Oh, I'm not sad, I'm pissed off. That bastard, he"—she groaned—"Brucie was a misogynistic douche—there, I said it! Not only because he used women for sex either. And it's why the idiot died. If he'd shut his big trap for once, he'd be here. But, no, Brucie had to be the hero and save the damsel in distress." A scoff escaped her lips. "I was fine, I didn't need to be rescued. That macho jerk"—a metallic bang echoed as Janice punched the wall—"just thinking about the freaking asshole makes me sick. Excuse me, I'm gonna throw up." Then she spun around and began walking away at a fast pace.

After a moment of stunned silence, Rose scowled. "That... was weird."

"Um, yeah."

Daniel shrugged. "No, I disagree." Though Rose fired an inquisitive glance, Daniel declined to explain and instead said, "Never mind, you wouldn't understand. I better go talk to her."

Once her father left, Rose turned toward James and forced a smile. "Okay, that happened. What a rough day. How are you holding up, Hunter?"

"Um, not great. I'm tired and..." James grimaced. "And Brucie... uh, I met him a few months ago and I feel like crap. You knew him for years, I can't imagine how you feel right now."

"Well, it's not poetic, but like crap is a fine description." Rose hesitated. "Hunter, I thought we'd lost you forever. Diabo threatened to take you. How did you escape?"

"That woman saved me. She's with BBR. They call her Wrath, uh"—James snapped his fingers—"something."

"Wrathchild..." If Rose's voice had failed to convey disdain, the way she gritted her teeth would have cleared up any potential confusion.

"Yes, that's it. Wrathchild untied me during the boxing match and hid me in a closet. She said she'd rather not have me tortured. When I appeared in Nirnivia, she saved me from the angry mob too." A blush reddened James's cheeks. "I guess that doesn't count since she brought me to Diabo, but deep down, I think she's a good person."

"Good person?" A derisive laugh resounded as Rose shook her head. Then she poked James's sternum with her index finger and he gulped. "Don't you dare defend that monster! Wrathchild's a terrorist, nothing more."

Rose was furious, so I figured something bad had happened between them. Discussing Diabo or even Doctor Death never made her that mad. I would have dropped the subject, but Wrathchild had asked a favor. Not much, just a short message for Rose. While I assumed she'd refuse to hear it, I had given my word.

—Thoughts of James Hunter, Hocmar 28, 2134, on the Nirnivian calendar

"Um... Rose... I... well... uh"—he winced—"she wanted me to tell you something."

"Forget it, I'm not interested."

"Please, Rose, I promised." Rose sighed and signaled for James to proceed. "Okay, so, she said she wished to explain everything, but there wasn't any time. Also, she's sorry and never meant to hurt you."

"Oh really?" Again, Rose let out a contemptuous chuckle. "So Wrathchild's begging for forgiveness. No, I can't give her that. People make mistakes, but enough is enough. Hunter, you have no idea what kind of person she is. Wrathchild committed crime after crime, each more heinous than the last. When I met her, I believed like you that deep down there was good in her. Because of this, I was the only one who gave her a chance. Nobody else would. For my efforts, she used me, then betrayed me and Nirnivia." Rose gazed into James's eyes and adopted a wretched smile. "I understand you're grateful, Hunter, and I am too. I offer her my deepest thanks for rescuing you, but that doesn't erase her sins. Here's a piece of advice: if you see Wrathchild again, don't turn your back on her or she might drive her sword through your chest."

I wasn't about to argue since I didn't care about Wrathchild that much. Besides, she was with BBR and that made her an enemy. Instead, we reminisced about Brucie. Rose told me stories. That brought depressing memories, but it was important.

—Thoughts of James Hunter, Hocmar 28, 2134, on the Nirnivian calendar

Chapter 9

Because of Daniel's late start, he lost sight of Janice, but he had an idea where she'd headed. His suspicion was confirmed when he entered the gym. There stood his daughter, striking a punching bag with all her might. The sack filled with rags and sand recoiled with every blow, accompanied by a moan from Janice. For a minute or two, Daniel stayed back and observed. Witnessing her train always impressed him given the considerable physical prowess and brute strength being displayed. Even in his prime, Janice had him beat. While Daniel enjoyed admiring her skills, it didn't serve as the main reason for the delay. He failed to find the proper words and so he waited, hoping inspiration would strike. When it didn't, he realized he just had to jump in and pray for the best.

That in mind, Daniel stepped forward and said, "I admire how you deal with frustration. Instead of yelling and screaming like an idiot, you build muscles. It's win-win."

Janice remained silent, though Daniel spotted a scowl forming on her brow as the jabs increased in frequency. Perhaps the greeting annoyed her rather than opening the path for further discussion. Ah well.

"Sweetie, I know you're taking Brucie's death hard."

Janice scoffed. "Really? Why would I? Brucie was a sexist asshole. Oh, that girl got captured; no way she can handle it on her own. Time for the sexy macho idiot to come to the rescue!" As she gritted her teeth, she fired a punch so powerful the bag flew off its hook and landed on the floor with a thud. After a short glance at the poor piece of equipment, Daniel nodded.

"Listen, sweetie, you have a point, but I don't think you're mad at Brucie."

"Oh yeah?" The sarcasm in Janice's tone proved clear. "So, who am I pissed at?" Janice wiped the sweat off her brow. "Ah, whatever, forget it. How about leaving me alone and go bug the princess like you usually do?"

"Okay, fine, I've been a crummy dad sometimes, and I'm sorry. But for once I'll do my job right. Janice, I understand how you feel."

Janice rolled her eyes. "Cut the bullshit."

"No BS here." Daniel sighed. "Do you have any idea how many people I've lost under my command? Just because they were following my orders. Like anyone, I make mistakes, and in my case the consequences are deadly." He lowered his gaze. "Sometimes, I even knowingly sent soldiers to their death because the situation called for it."

"Shut up and freaking get out of here!"

"Believe it or not, that's been rough on your old dad. I don't know how many sleepless nights I spent tossing and turning in bed, but there's been plenty." A sob escaped Daniel's lips. "To this day, I see their faces when I close my eyes. They've been piling up through the years, and I'm still adding more."

"I said shut up!"

"But that's the nature of the job. I had no choice except try to forgive myself and keep going."

"Stop before I kill you."

Daniel chuckled. "Nah, I'll take the risk." With that, he rested his palm on her shoulder. Though Janice shuddered at the touch, she declined to shove his arm away. "Sweetie, what happened to Brucie wasn't your fault. The mission failed, but you did your best. Besides, it was his own decision, so the blame isn't yours."

Then Janice whimpered and pushed Daniel, breaking contact. While she no doubt intended a light nudge, thanks to her formidable strength, it sent Daniel a few paces away, and he almost tumbled backward.

"You're wrong!" She glared at him. "I didn't try my best! I could have killed Allison, but I hesitated because I pitied her. And after Charlie sacrificed himself because he trusted me." On that note, Janice sat down, holding her head with both hands.

"I see. As the Commander, I wish you had pulled the trigger." Daniel joined Janice on the floor and wrapped his arm around her. "But as a father, I'm glad that even after suffering through war, my daughter has enough compassion to have mercy for a poor abused woman who did nothing wrong. I'm sure Brucie would have felt the same way."

The instant Daniel finished that sentence, tears started rolling down her cheeks. Janice rested her head against Daniel's shoulder and soon his uniform grew wet. "God damn you, Brucie!" The sobs doubled. "The bastard made me break my promise again!" That declaration caused Daniel's own eyes to water. He shifted position and hugged Janice. Against the odds, she hugged back. "I miss him so much, Dad."

"I know, sweetie. Everyone does."

Chapter 10

With the celebration party for Plague's return long over, most of BBR's crew fell into slumber. The crimson beast himself, Diabo, passed out drunk even with the resistance to alcohol offered by his gigantic size. Despite this, however, Plague and Stalker remained up. Tucked in a deep dark corner of the cave functioning as their current hideout, they discussed the rescue mission in private. Given their comrade's inebriated state, they could have done so without retiring to a less conspicuous spot, but because of the contents of their conversation, Plague insisted out of caution.

A bottle in hand, Stalker poured himself a serving of uisge and downed it the instant he filled his shot glass. Plague expected the quality to be far inferior to the brand rumor claimed Daniel Ricdeau stashed in his office against regulations. Not that he tested it. Alcohol left his ravaged body aching and sickened, so he abstained. The same failed to hold true for Stalker. The master of camouflage had drunk so much by this point that the fact he remained standing astonished Plague. "Uh, you've been hitting the stuff hard. How 'bout giving it a rest for tonight?"

After a groan, Stalker dismissed the suggestion with a wave. "Nah, I'm good. Heh, after the crap Diabo pulled today I need it." On that note, he began pouring another round, only to change his mind and take a sip from the bottle instead. "That goddamn idiot. Can you believe him? He thinks he was smart. His stunt told NISDA exactly what to expect. The bastard could have gotten me killed. Why the freak would distracting the freaking Commander help me out, anyway? Even when he's cautious, he's reckless."

A nod came from Plague. "Yeah, I know. Good thing my story convinced Hal to join us, or we'd be screwed. Diabo is becoming a liability."

"Oh yeah?" Stalker forced a humorless chuckle. "If ya ask me, he's been one for a while."

"You're right, and he's not getting better."

"Are you finally ready to do something about it?"

Plague closed his eyes and sighed. "Listen, I told you before, I can't take over. I'm too messed up to be the boss. Don't worry, I've been drafting plans for a while. I'll figure it out."

"Sure hope so." Stalker sampled his beverage once more. "Better be before he gets us all killed."

"I'll try my best." That response brought a frown out of Stalker, and Plague laughed. "Just kidding, we'll be fine."

Chapter 11

Daniel thanked God this cursed day was over. This one had been tough all around. The negotiations had proven stressful enough, but then Plague had escaped with the help of a traitor. That brought a whole new set of headaches Daniel had to handle. And that wasn't even considering Brucie's death. At least Doug and Jade had called and congratulated him on saving most hostages, though he'd had little impact on that outcome. At any rate, Daniel needed to decompress, and the same held true for Ron, who joined him in his office for this purpose. As soon as he sat at his desk, Daniel grabbed a shot glass and the hidden uisge bottle. Without delay, he poured himself a serving of the golden liquid. As he did so, Tigh eyed the glass.

"Damn, that's tempting. You're not helping me fight my demons, Dan."

"Oh, how insensitive of me." Daniel sighed. "Sorry, Ron." With that, Daniel dropped the alcohol back in the container and put it out of view.

The Koporal dismissed the apology with a wave. "Bah, it's not like I usually give a shit."

"Sure, but these are special circumstances."

"Yeah, you could say that. Diabo played us for chumps! Freaking Diabo! I can understand when Doctor Death fools us, but that idiot?" A groan escaped Tigh. "We're losing our edge, old friend."

"Maybe so." Daniel paused for a second. "Poor Brucie. Rose is devastated, Janice blames herself. What a disaster."

"Could be worse. Imagine what Rose would do if it was the human kid who died. For crying out loud, Dan, she's spending all her free time with him. It makes me sick. Why did you allow the guy in here?"

"I told you before, it's for Rose's sake. She's depressed and James helps somehow. Nothing else does. As much as I hated it, I didn't dare refuse her request." A smile formed on Daniel's face. "Besides, you agreed to it."

"Yeah, yeah, I remember." Ron grimaced. "Rose's not my daughter and dear Ulgorack she pisses me off, but I saw her grow up, and"—Tigh moaned—"Dan, we're good guys and like always it'll bite us in the ass."

"Give James a chance, he's not that bad. I think he's a nice kid. You shouldn't judge him so quick: he's not the same as—"

The Koporal slapped the desk, interrupting him with a bang. "I know, okay! Look, I guess it means I'm a freaking speciesist, but I can't trust him. He makes my skin crawl."

"Oh, I don't blame you, he does the same to me."

Chapter 12

With a sad smile, Kristina watched Rose crumple another piece of paper. Similar failed attempts filled the wastebasket, and a few littered the floor. Kristina harrumphed and the Voice of God faced her. The sparks in Rose's eyes had vanished. That, plus their puffiness and the bags under them, confirmed her exhaustion. Even in this state, Rose's grace shone through and Kristina envied her beauty.

"Kristina? What are you doing here at this hour?"

Oh yes, it was late, far too late for Rose to still be awake after this stressful day. "I bring a gift." She approached holding a cup of coffee. "If you listen to my advice, you'll refuse it and go to bed. My guess is you'll keep working on your eulogy instead and so will need a pick-me-up."

"Thanks, I appreciate the gesture." Then Rose confirmed Kristina's suspicions by taking a sip. The bitter taste she so despised brought a grimace.

Kristina pointed at the overflowing trash can. "It's not progressing well?"

"Oh, it's horrible! I don't understand, I've written a thousand eulogies. Why is this one so difficult? I want it to be perfect—he deserves that—but so far, all I've done is pure drivel. It's Brucie, I should be inspired."

"Rose, you're a great orator. Don't try so hard."

A scowl formed on the prophet's brow. "The worst part is, I know what Brucie would want and yet when I write it... dear Ulgorack." Rose sighed and Kristina patted her shoulder.

"Speak from the heart and it'll be fine. Rose... I'm sorry for your loss. I... never connected with Brucie. I wasn't exactly nice to him. God, we were so incompatible, but he was a good man in his way and... oh, I wish I'd treated him better."

"Kristina, don't do this to yourself. Brucie wasn't easy to like. Sometimes he got on my nerves too. And he wasn't nice to you either."

"I guess not." She shuddered as she recalled that cafeteria incident from months ago.

Then silence fell, and the two women gazed at each other without a word until finally Rose said, "Kristina, thank you for everything. Go home and rest now. You've done enough."

"I could say the same to you, Rose. You should go to bed."

"I will. One final attempt, and I'll call it a day, I promise." Kristina didn't believe her, but she preferred not to insist. Resigned, she headed toward the door. At the last second, she stopped and glanced at the Melkar. Witnessing her so distraught pulled at Kristina's heartstrings. As a result, the weight of the secret she kept from the redheaded woman proved even heavier than usual. What if she revealed it, freeing herself from that burden? The notion covered her in a cold sweat, and yet...

"Rose?"

"Yes?" As Rose faced her, Kristina's resolve faded and only weakness remained. No, she lacked the strength. Anyway, it wasn't a proper time: Rose should deal with her grief first.

"Oh, nothing important. Good night." With that, Kristina left.

***

No matter how much I twisted and turned, I just couldn't fall asleep. After a while, I gave up and instead fetched Nadia's picture.

—Thoughts of James Hunter, Hocmar 28, 2134, on the Nirnivian calendar

Lying wide awake in his bed, James fixed his girlfriend's photo like he had so often since his arrival in Nirnivia. The smile on Nadia's face contrasted with his somber mood. That had happened countless times in previous conversations. No matter how dark the words that escaped his lips proved to be, Nadia's cheerful expression remained constant, a fact he could not blame a static image for.

"It's so unfair. Like, I don't know." James sighed. "For months now, I've been stuck here. I've been so alone, and I missed you so much. And everyone else too. Still, little by little, I grew used to this place and its faces, and now bang, one of them is gone. It's like—" A sob escaped him. "Everything changed and I'm back at square one again." With another whimper, James caressed Nadia's cheek with his index finger. "When I speak with you, it's the only time I feel like I have a home. At least you're not going anywhere."

Chapter 13

Valar 7, 2134, on the Nirnivian calendar

Several perished at the church of Onel and that meant fu-nerals. On Valar 7—God, I hate their month names—anyway, on Valar 7, it was Brucie's turn and Rose dreaded that day. She was expected to perform a eulogy, and it terrified her de-spite her experience. Whenever someone important passed away, like an esteemed politician, a great priest or a heroic soldier, she'd speak at the ceremony to honor them. However, mourning a stranger and mourning a close friend are two dif-ferent things. With Brucie, she feared she might not find the right words. I believed she'd do a wonderful job, but she doubted herself. She wished she could avoid it, but Brucie asked her in his will and Rose wouldn't deny his request. Be-sides, he deserved her praises. They held the funeral outside; he wanted it that way. The crowd gathered in a beautiful gar-den. Brucie didn't have many living relatives, but there were plenty of people present since he died a hero. Rose wasn't with them. She considered going even with the safety concerns, but then she decided putting herself at risk would go against eve-rything Brucie had worked for. Instead, she watched through video conference and I stayed behind with her in case she needed my support.

—Thoughts of James Hunter, Hocmar 28, 2134, on the Nirnivian calendar

James stood by Rose's side as they observed Brucie's memorial on the screen. The black dress she had chosen suited the occasion but unsettled him. In the past, the prophet had only worn a particular white dress, a training outfit, or her pajamas. That dress proved so significant, she possessed numerous copies. The instant Rose appeared in front of the camera, the crowd began whispering among themselves. Though he had no way of hearing them, James expected the unfamiliar clothing served as the cause. Rose opened her mouth to speak but froze. For a moment that morphed into an eternity, she remained silent. As he squeezed her hand, James murmured words of encouragement in her ear.

Rose offered a grateful smile and then said, "Everyone, I..." She paused and sobbed. A couple seconds passed, and she tried again, "This is irregular, but I must apologize. I am reputed for my eloquence, but I am unsure if I will perform my duties adequately. I might even cry. Please, forgive me. Brucie was a dear friend and I am afraid his death is difficult for me. Actually, I must apologize for this too. People feel sadder when a loved one passes away compared to a stranger. That's true for everyone and I suppose not surprising. Yet as the Melkar, I'm to be objective. All lives are sacred, thus all deaths are equal. Friend, stranger, hero or criminal, it doesn't matter: for Ulgorack, every life has the same value.

"That concept goes further: in reality, death shouldn't pain us since it is an essential step to reach the afterlife and a well-deserved rest. The Melkar should understand this better than anyone else, but here I am mourning my deceased bodyguard. I have performed several eulogies before, but this one is particularly demanding. Today, I have failed you and I am sorry. I guess, despite my role, I am still a woman with her weaknesses..."

James refused to blame her for that, and as he studied the assembly, he assumed they agreed. The majority nodded in sympathy. Rose put unrealistic pressure on her shoulders. "Now, I should address my clothing. I noticed it came as a shock. To wear black at funerals is tradition, but the holy prophet is above such customs. Most expected the habitual white dress. I debated the issue and grief trumped duty, so I must apologize again." She sighed. "But, enough excuses."

Before proceeding, Rose cleared her throat and moved a strand of hair. From his point of view, James realized the motion concealed a tear that had fallen on her cheek. "I was fortunate to meet Mr. Brucie Garland when I did. He saved my life and almost lost his in the process. That's not surprising. There are plenty who would sacrifice themselves for the Melkar's sake. However, it was unexpected from Brucie. During his younger years, he made several mistakes and earned the reputation of being an irresponsible clown. Then the charity incident happened. As a mere spectator, Brucie had no obligation, but he protected me and received a bullet in return. That changed everything, and the clown became a hero.

"When I visited him at the hospital, I learned of Brucie's past, how his father abandoned his family and the ensuing financial burden. Because of this, I offered him a position as a bodyguard and the proper training. People questioned my decision, and I doubted he'd be effective myself, but I figured it didn't matter given I had tons of experienced bodyguards. One thing was for certain: I never regretted hiring Brucie. I won't pretend he was perfect; nobody is, and Brucie had his share of flaws. While he was considered a hero, many didn't like him on a personal level. I can understand why. Brucie could be obnoxious; his jokes were unfunny and could be grating, not to mention on occasion they were downright mean. Beyond that, he made plenty of women cry, and I won't deny the accusations of misogyny are understandable. While I can't condone some of his actions, you must realize Brucie never wished to hurt anyone. Because of that, I can forgive his transgressions and I hope those he hurt during his short life will do the same."

Rose took a deep breath and shivered. "Brucie and I shared our happiest and saddest moments. Though we were close, an invisible wall stood between us. I know he often yearned to confide in me but didn't because of my status. Still, for years he was perhaps the only one I could call a friend. Our friendship didn't reach its full potential because of his faith, but I will cherish it till I'm gone. At first, Brucie puzzled me. He joked about everything. When tragedy struck, he kidded around as if nothing happened."

A sad laugh escaped Rose's lips. "I can't count the number of occasions his apparent callousness offended someone. Such incidents implied he didn't care about anything, but I swear that wasn't the case. Brucie cared about people, and he had a strong sense of duty that went beyond dedication. With the war, we contemplated hiring additional bodyguards, but there was no need thanks to him. Nobody asked Brucie to work harder. He did it out of pure devotion. If you won't believe me when I say Brucie cared about people, consider his demise. He sacrificed himself to rescue the hostages. Though his plan failed, that doesn't lessen his valor. The question remains, why all the jokes? Once I learned a family member was sick, and he joked about it! That was so cruel, and it made me so furious I refused to talk to Brucie for weeks."

Rose sobbed. "Eventually, I figured him out and I will provide the answer. Brucie loved life, and he deemed it too short to waste on tears. He wanted everyone to enjoy themselves. So, rather than bow to tragedy, he laughed in its face. During all those years, I witnessed events so terrible that they crushed Brucie's spirit, though those were few. I'll admit that his way of thinking might not always have been appropriate. Sometimes his efforts brought more pain and not the intended relief. And it didn't help that Brucie wasn't that funny. Oh, he tried hard—too hard—but his humor often fell flat. He lacked a gift for comedy, which is probably why he ended up a bodyguard. Beyond that, I'm not sure I agree with his basic philosophy, but that does not change the fact that Brucie had a huge heart even if it wasn't always clear."

A slight pause as she indulged in a whimper. "You know, Brucie would hate this funeral. It's gloomy and he would despise that. He would not want us to cry for him. On the contrary, he'd want us to party and have fun. If he had his wish, this eulogy would be a comedy act, and I'd end with a hilarious joke that would have you burst into laughter for hours." Another silence followed. Rose had struggled to keep the tears at bay so far, but at that instant she lost the battle and couldn't stop them anymore. "And so, I have to apologize again, this time to Brucie himself. I am sorry, Brucie, I cannot laugh today. I'm torn up inside. I'm sorry... there won't be any big joke finish. I'm sorry, Brucie, for not giving you your wish. I tried... I wrote through the night, but... I can't do it, I just can't. I'm sorry, Brucie, but right now all I can do is weep."

With that, it was over. I can't speak for anyone else, but she moved me. Maybe I'm kidding myself, but based on the faces on the screen, I think I wasn't alone. After that ordeal, Rose was tired and weak, so I helped her walk to her room. Once there, we sat on her bed and talked.

—Thoughts of James Hunter, Hocmar 28, 2134, on the Nirnivian calendar

"You did great!" James said. "It was beautiful."

"Thank you, but it's still not the eulogy Brucie would have liked."

"Oh, he'd understand. You're not him, you can't act like him." He winced. "It's funny, I often hated Brucie's stupid jokes, but now that he's gone, I'd give anything to hear one more."

"I'm the same way. Hunter, I've seen so many deaths in my life—so much suffering. One would think I'd be used to it, but somehow it becomes worse and worse. I just... will we ever be all right? I'm not sure I can get over it."

"You will. We'll live on, Rose. We'll keep on going, because that's what Brucie would want us to do."

And so we did. At first, it was difficult; it felt like things would never be the same. And I guess they weren't. After a while it became easier. Routine settled in, and yet the wound didn't fully heal. I still miss Brucie today. Hell, I could use a good joke or two right now. Okay, so Brucie wasn't the one to go to for a good joke, but at least he'd try.

—Thoughts of James Hunter, Hocmar 28, 2134, on the Nirnivian calendar

The Broken Knight

Chapter 1

Valar 9, 2134, on the Nirnivian calendar

Cheers filled the room as Gareth raised his glass along with the other soldiers. A second later, he gulped down the contents and indulged in a satisfied grunt. He had been selected for his first mission since his return to service, and his colleagues had organized a soiree to celebrate. Well, that wasn't a hundred percent accurate. Others would join him, and the party was meant for all of them. Still, given Gareth's long hiatus from active duty, most considered him the guest of honor.

"So, when do you guys leave?" someone named Bran asked.

Patricia shrugged. "We're not sure. According to current intel, about a month, but that can change."

"The bigwigs are planning ahead. Must be an important one."

Then Gareth detected movement on his right and turned his head. A black-haired man he recognized as Ken Marcella smirked. "You guys'll make the Ostarkiran bastards bleed for me, won't you?"

Those words reminded Gareth that the poor fellow had lost his wife when Ostark had bombed the Orontian launchpad, a tragedy brought on by that goddamn strike. He forced a chuckle. "Sorry, it's a stealth mission, so don't count on it."

"Ah, too bad. Oh well, keep an eye out in case an opportunity presents itself."

***

Later that evening, the crowd thinned out. A few soldiers still loitered in Yvan's living room, including their host, but most had left already. Working for NISDA implied waking early. Gareth himself considered heading home. He grew sleepy and had had his fill of alcohol. As that thought entered his mind, he spotted Janice Ricdeau approaching him. The gigantic woman's movements lacked energy and the bags under her eyes suggested a lack of sleep. Brucie's death, not to mention Charlie's, weighed on her, Gareth realized.

"Janice," he began in a soft tone. "I'm so sorry for your loss. I know Brucie meant a lot to you."

"Thanks." She bit her lip. "Buddy, make sure you come back alive. I don't want to add you to the list."

"Don't worry, I will. I swear I'm better now. I have no intention of dying."

"Good."

With that they hugged and, once the embrace relented, shared the secret handshake their squad had adopted during the old war.

***

Valar 10, 2134, on the Nirnivian calendar

The following days were difficult. It was as if Brucie's shadow lingered everywhere. Constant sadness weighed on us. Despite this, we kept going. Rose was still the Melkar and a councillor, so she had to perform her duties. She could've had used a break, but no luck there. Me, I spent most of my time alone and it didn't help me cope. A variety of soldiers guarded Rose until they hired an official bodyguard. They were dis-

creet, and I didn't get to know any of them on a personal level. Rose stopped exercising for a short while, but soon she tried. It was... different. No Brucie to cheer her on or mess with me. Yeah, he could be annoying, but he'd grown on me. While Rose had trained without Brucie when he was injured, this was a lot worse because he'd never return.

—Thoughts of James Hunter, Hocmar 28, 2134, on the Nirnivian calendar

Though Rose attempted to keep the strict regimen imposed by Brucie, James realized her heart wasn't in it. Each exercise she performed for a shorter duration than usual. A few of the most strenuous ones she outright skipped. Her speed also dropped. The soldier escorting Rose, while vigilant, remained silent, offering neither encouragement nor comments on her performance. In fact, he proved so quiet that once or twice James forgot about his presence until the guy entered his field of vision and he recoiled in shock.

Before long, Rose finished. The session lasted at least fifteen minutes less than when overseen by Brucie. Regardless, perspiration covered her skin and dampened her hair. No doubt she needed a shower, but first she sat next to James for a quick chat. A whiff of faint body odor tickled his nostrils, but he tried his best to keep a neutral expression.

Rose lowered her neck. "It's not the same at all."

A nod came from James. "No, it's not."

"Hunter, this place reminds me so much of Brucie." She frowned. "It demanded all my strength not to collapse on the ground and cry."

"Um, I know what you mean." James scratched behind his head. "I feel the same way."

"I can't do this anymore. So many sad memories..." A sigh escaped Rose's lips. "But I can't stop. I'd get sloppy."

"Maybe it's too soon?"

"I guess so."

***

As Daniel finished reading the transcription of Ed's latest communication, he rested the paper on his desk. Then he gazed at Tigh, who sat on the opposite side.

"Ed confirms the machine is in Nerboros. He saw it with his own eyes."

"Hmm, that's weird." Tigh rubbed his chin. "It's a month earlier than expected, I don't like it."

"According to Ed, the specialist they asked to help had a sudden schedule change and so they had to push up the date." Daniel shrugged. "Seems legit. I mean, they'd never move the thing to a third-rate facility if the guy had proper clearance, so it makes sense they're accommodating him."

"Yeah, but I have a bad feeling. That Ed guy's a fruitcake, and now our preparation time's cut short."

A nod came from Daniel. "Yes, that's annoying, but it's fine. We already have a plan and a team ready to head for Nerboros."

Ron scoffed. "If you say so, but damn, after that church business I could've used a longer break before the next big one."

"Oh, I agree, but on the bright side, since we're busy and useful, the Council won't get rid of us."

"Heh, yeah, as if that'd ever happen. We got job security, old friend." The Koporal sighed. "At least there won't be any freaking hostages, and this time we're the ones on the offensive. Better hope we don't piss off the Doc again, though."

Daniel nodded. "That'd be a problem, but if worse comes to worst, it'll be okay. Like I said before, if he didn't restart the war when we tried to kill him, he won't over this." He joined his fingers in a pyramid. "Let's just pray our luck turns around. Our track record's been lousy lately."

***

Valar 11, 2134, on the Nirnivian calendar

I was watching a boring show on TV when the doorbell rang. I opened the door and found Kristina Dupree. That surprised me—our relationship had improved, but she didn't visit unless she sought Rose. She looked worried and immediately explained that I should go see Rose as soon as possible, so I rushed over there.

—Thoughts of James Hunter, Hocmar 28, 2134, on the Nirnivian calendar

After two or three pushes of the interphone's button, Rose let James inside her quarters. The instant he entered, the prophet headed for the bed and sat on the mattress. Based on her puffy red eyes, James deduced she'd been crying a lot. Several pictures lay around Rose, though he couldn't tell what they portrayed from his position.

"Are you all right?" James asked, his voice filled with concern.

"I've been better..." With that, Rose waved for him to approach and he joined her. The distance now closed, James realized the photos depicted a handsome blond man sporting deep blue eyes glimmering with confidence. Though it took a second, he recognized Miguel, Rose's deceased husband. Based on his charm and physical attributes, James expected Miguel had been popular with the fairer sex. No wonder Rose had fallen for him.

With a sigh, Rose gestured toward the images. "I guess I'm torturing myself. I just... Brucie's death reminded me of him."

"Um, I understand."

"I know I shouldn't have, I'm hurting myself. How stupid of me."

"No, don't say that. You're not stupid—you're in pain. How about we get out of here? Let's go to the rec room and try to have fun."

Rose frowned. "I don't feel like having fun."

"Yeah, me neither. But sometimes, that's when you need it the most."

She reluctantly agreed. As we left, I glanced at the pictures. There was a variety of them, including one from their wedding and another where Rose wore a sexy bikini at the beach. Okay, I'll admit that was a pleasant view, but a different photo grabbed my attention: Rose and Miguel stood before some sort of ruins—maybe the remains of an ancient civilization. Don't ask me why, but it gave me shivers. I had more pressing concerns, so I didn't dwell on it.

—Thoughts of James Hunter, Hocmar 28, 2134, on the Nirnivian calendar

***

Valar 12, 2134, on the Nirnivian calendar

Rose and I sat in the cafeteria. Meals weren't the same either without Brucie. Unlike training, we couldn't avoid food, though. As I enjoyed the familiar mediocre taste, I noted the strange atmosphere. There was something unpleasant in the air; I couldn't quite put my finger on it.

—Thoughts of James Hunter, Hocmar 28, 2134, on the Nirnivian calendar

"So, Hunter, how are you holding up?" Rose asked after a quick bite.

James grimaced. "Um, I still feel like crap. How about you?"

"Same. And to make matters worse, I've got a Council meeting this afternoon."

"Really? What about?"

Rose shrugged. "Oh, I'm not even sure. I don't have the energy to keep up. No doubt something boring and pointless. Politics is often like that." She groaned. "I hate it, but at least it distracts me from... well, you know."

"Yeah, I guess so."

As I said those words, I spotted Janice in the distance. It was the first time I'd seen her since we'd returned from the church. She didn't look too great. Messy hair, dark circles around her eyes. I waved at her; so did Rose. While Janice waved back, she stayed far away. Actually, I think she left because she didn't want to speak to us.

—Thoughts of James Hunter, Hocmar 28, 2134, on the Nirnivian calendar

"I hope she's okay," James mumbled.

"Me too." A scowl formed on Rose's brow. "From what Dad told me, Janice's better now. I don't know for certain. She isn't keeping in touch with me."

"Yeah." After an instant of hesitation, James frowned. "Rose, the mood around here is, uh, different."

"Oh? Well, it's a difficult time..."

"No, I don't mean that. Everyone's so nervous."

The redheaded prophet nodded. "You're perceptive, Hunter. All right, since you're curious, I'll tell you. There's a military operation in progress and it's a big one. Everyone is worried. I can't give more details. National security, you understand?"

"That's fine. I think I'm better off in the dark anyway."

Chapter 2

Valar 13, 2134, on the Nirnivian calendar

As she watched her sister, Anya sank her teeth into her sandwich for another bite. It proved lackluster, but she'd expected that much. Being in a rush, she'd thrown together a lunch at the last minute with stale bread and generic cold cuts she'd found in the fridge. A poor excuse for a meal, but she promised herself she'd make up for it when dinner came along.

On the opposite side of the table, Tania hadn't even touched her food yet. Instead, she rubbed her chin while talking about their current project. This was standard behavior for her. When a scientific challenge presented itself, Tania's mind refused to focus on anything else. "I don't understand. The best explanation for his symptoms is still an allergic reaction."

"But you said it yourself—the graft was synthesized from his own skin cells. The nanomachines duplicated them perfectly; he'd have to be allergic to himself."

"Yeah, but nothing else panned out, I'm running out of potential explanations." Tania clicked her tongue. "What about an allergy to Banzeine?"

Poor Tania was going around in circles. Anya had already considered Banzeine even before she'd enlisted her sibling's help. As a chemical produced by nanomachines during the synthetization process, it served as a likely cause. And though rare, allergies existed, explaining why some patients couldn't receive nanomachine injections to treat injuries. "You know we filter out the Banzeine—there's no trace left. Why, we tested it on allergic people and they were fine."

"Yes, I'm just saying whatever pops into my head." Tania sighed. "I'm at a loss. At this rate, it'll take us weeks!" With a cheerful yelp, she pumped her fist. "What a challenge. This is so awesome!"

A sad smile formed on Anya's lips. "Maybe the poor sap with the rash doesn't feel the same."

Tania dismissed the notion with a wave. "Ah, he's okay, the rash is gone already."

While an urge to chastise her sister for her lack of compassion presented itself, Anya declined to. For Tania, science and equations came before people, a fact she had no choice but to learn to accept.

***

As Rose rubbed her head, she paced around her room. By sheer determination, she resisted chewing her nails. That bad habit had returned during the hostage crisis, but she intended to banish it once more. Then again, she doubted she'd succeeded. The current stress level she endured almost broke her, and it would grow with each passing second.

Since Rose realized today would be nerve-wracking, she took the day off. To her, attempting to work when her mind wouldn't be able to focus seemed pointless. But that might've been a mistake. Yes, she'd have given an atrocious performance, to the point her that presence could've slowed down Kristina rather than helped her, but waiting in her chamber alone drove her insane, while work might have distracted her from the matter at hand. Stuck on her own, the coming event's implications kept circling inside her brain. She needed guidance but lacked any. Everyone was busy, or had already offered their opinion. Well, except Hunter, she supposed. How she wished to visit him and talk about her torments, but this time she couldn't turn to her human friend. Even a game of Kuhard proved impossible. The simple thought brought shudders. While she rejected seeking James's company, Rose glanced in the mirror.

The instant the looking glass entered her vision, Rose shuddered. A voice in her head warned her to stay away. Whatever that thing wished to say would be to her detriment. Yet, what other option remained? She'd discussed her doubts and guilt with everybody except herself. With a sigh, she sat at her desk and gazed into her duplicate's eyes. The reflection stared back in silence.

"Please help me," Rose whispered.

A large smile formed on the image's lips. Though friendly in appearance, it sent a shiver down Rose's spine. "Long time no see. I suppose you were once again ignoring me." The reversed prophet squinted. "Oh my, you look terrible. Why such a sad face?"

"Because I—" Rose moaned. "If he somehow finds out, will he ever forgive me?"

A shrug came as the answer. "I am sorry, for I cannot tell. Whether or not he does depends much on him. I would suggest you prepare an apology. It cannot do any harm."

"Am I—" Rose swallowed hard. "Am I a horrible person?"

"Difficult, difficult questions you ask today. Judging someone's character is a complex matter. There are so many variables. Unfortunately, I cannot provide an absolute answer, but for what it's worth, you believe so." Cuts opened on the reflection's face as if slashed by an invisible knife. Blood dripped, covering her body and staining the white dress. The background morphed into a sea of flames. "Why else would you yearn to burn for your sins?"

"Stop it!" Rose covered her eyes with her hand. Her breathing sped up. Why did she do this? What did she expect would happen? Exactly this, yet she tried anyway. In the past, breaking visual contact had stopped the illusion, but this time it persevered, and in a warning tone, it said, "You can close your ears, but it matters not, for they keep singing the hymns and destruction ensues. To vanquish the chaos, you must recognize their song. However, there is a price to pay. Perhaps it is too great." Riddles; always riddles. Rose cursed herself for succumbing to her mirror's temptation. The strange conversations only brought confusion and sorrow. Rose got up, walked to her bed and collapsed in it. There she wept as she had so often before. On her pillow lay her childhood doll, Ms. Penny. Rose grabbed her in a hug, staining the white fabric with tears.

***

Familiar situation: Rose was busy, so I was alone. I tried my best to occupy myself. After breakfast, I hung out in the rec room, hoping Janice or Patricia might show up for a game of Rubarg. They didn't. Eventually, I returned to my quarters and watched TV. Since there wasn't anything interesting on, I soon turned to my minicomp instead.

—Thoughts of James Hunter, Hocmar 28, 2134, on the Nirnivian calendar

Stylus in hand, James dragged the colored jewels across the board. The touchscreen lacked responsiveness, but through practice he'd learned its quirks and compensated.

In an explosion, the three linked green gems vanished, causing those on top to collapse, and more trios connected. This led to a chain reaction, or combo, and for his reward, James received a ton of points. Though he hoped to maintain the pace and feared running out of time, James risked glancing at his score. Over 130,000. Soon, he'd beat his record. Any simple match would do. And there, he found one. The tip of his stylus scraped the misaligned stone. Nothing happened. James repeated the gesture, to no effect. He scratched his head and scowled. Then he noticed the timer had stopped. The freaking minicomp had frozen.

Once James let out a few curses, he decided a hard reboot proved necessary. That would reset his progress, but he saw no other solution. His finger reached for the power button. Before he touched it, the screen flashed and gray static filled it. Along with the distortion, a hissing sound echoed through the speakers, making James grimace. Then the image cleared up, the pleasant game replaced by a robotic figure.

"Hello again, James," Doctor Death said as he offered a slight bow. "Please forgive the intrusion, but it is imperative we have a chat."

James gritted his teeth. "I'm not interested! I've had enough of you. Yeah, Rose lied about the first human and other things, but I don't care anymore. It doesn't matter if you're from earth. There are plenty of assholes over there and you're just one of them. But Rose... I, uh"—the memories of the traumatic event flooded his mind and James choked—"was a hostage recently."

"Yes, I am aware. I wish I could have helped. Alas, I learned of your predicament after the fact."

A grunt came from James. "Whatever. The point is it made me realize how much I mean to Rose and how much she means to me. You should've seen the fear in her eyes when Diabo threatened me. Rose even offered to sacrifice herself. She cares a hell of a lot about me. Listen, I don't know why you're trying to tear us apart, but it won't work. I'm done with you."

The mechanical man nodded. "Of course Rose cares about you, James. You are her best friend. I never intended to suggest otherwise. If I gave the wrong impression, I apologize." That brought a twitch out of James. "However, that does not change the fact that you are in potential danger. Rose is fond of you, but if you ever became a nuisance, you would be disposed of in a most foul manner."

"Look, I have enough shit in my life right now without you adding more."

"Ah, you are referring to Mr. Garland's death, are you not?" The smiling face inside the president's electronic eye morphed into a sad one. "I offer my sincere sympathy. What happened in that church is a tragedy. Alas, such is Diabo's folly. I met Brucie before I became this mechanical monstrosity. I will not pretend we were close. Oh no, the truth is we often clashed." He shook his head. "Despite this, I never wished him ill. If I could bring Brucie back, I swear I would. Resurrection is beyond my capabilities at the moment. Perhaps in the future, though it is unlikely."

"Keep your sympathy to yourself! Leave me alone. I've heard enough of your lies. I don't even care if Rose is the villain! This isn't my world, and it's not my business." Without further ado, James pushed the start button. Five seconds and the minicomp would shut down. In silence he counted. Five... four... three... two... one...

Nothing. Puzzled, James pressed it again.

"Uh, what the hell?"

The Doctor snapped his fingers. "Oh yes, I forgot to mention you cannot end this call."

"But... but, um, that's impossible."

"You are incorrect. If it was impossible, then it would not be happening." The cyborg shrugged. "That minicomp has quirks allowing this trick. I would explain in detail, but it is technical and boring. Beside, we have a lot to discuss. Fear not, I have taken special precautions so we can talk for longer than usual."

So I couldn't hang up. Don't ask me how Doctor Death managed that, but it didn't force me to listen. I could have removed the battery, except I didn't have a screwdriver. But that didn't stop me from smashing my minicomp. Or, less drastically, stashing it somewhere until he gave up. Yeah, I had several options, but I didn't use any of them. I guess I wanted to hear what he had to say even if I wouldn't admit it.

—Thoughts of James Hunter, Hocmar 28, 2134, on the Nirnivian calendar

Chapter 3

As he walked alongside his three companions, Gareth reflected about how he hated his clothes. The NISDA uniform he had grown used to wearing was made of a thick, strong fabric, while the lab coat and pants he wore now proved less than robust, which made him feel vulnerable. Then again, arriving at Nerboros dressed like enemy soldiers would have meant certain death. Besides, the goal was to avoid fights and fulfill the mission without detection. Given those orders, even the sturdiest body armor wouldn't help.

Soon, Gareth and his colleagues reached their destination. Nerboros served as a third-rate research center operated by the Ostarkiran government. Since it wasn't a military facility, little of interest to NISDA happened there. Under normal circumstances, infiltrating the place would have been a futile endeavor. That had changed when Ed Drebin, a new Nirnivian spy, discovered that Doctor Death had ordered a special device transferred there. At first, everyone doubted the intel. After further investigation, it had ended up being accurate, and the top brass had decided to act.

Despite the relative lack of security at Nerboros, entry required passing through a checkpoint. There, guards verified your ID card, performed a pat-down and made you pass through a metal detector. Nothing too scary. Plus, those guys weren't Ostarkiran soldiers but mere rent-a-cops types that failed to intimidate Gareth. The line, however, annoyed him. He estimated it'd take around ten, fifteen minutes before their turn. Still, that was a minor inconvenience.

As Gareth waited, he glanced at his three colleagues. Behind him stood Patricia, a Perz who enjoyed playing video games and Rubarg. While he deemed his lab coat geeky, it suited her and conveyed an impression of intelligence. As for the two men trailing them, Yvan had inherited an average body and a face people often forgot, so he blended into the scenery without a problem. Fermin, however... the tall and large soldier with his black hair arranged in a ponytail didn't resemble the stereotypical researcher. Thank Ulgorack the scientists broke with preconceived notions and came in various shapes and sizes. That mitigated the issue, but Fermin drew surprised glances regardless. That might cause trouble as even Gareth's facial scars gained less attention. He supposed they'd find out.

Before long, Gareth reached the checkpoint, and the guard presented him with a scanning device. A flash of the old war involving a similar situation that had ended in a shoot-out popped into his mind, but he blocked it out. Thank you, Dr. Crane. As demanded, Gareth slid his ID card into the proper slot. Less than a second later, a green light flashed, accompanied by an approving beep. A smile began forming on his lips, but he concealed it. Displaying unwarranted happiness here could raise suspicion. That test passed, he lifted his arms as instructed, and they let the sentry run his hands over him. Occasionally, the touch wandered into unpleasant areas. Though Gareth endured worse to enter Valardir, his body urged him to retaliate. Somehow he resisted the temptation. Then the guard asked him to remove any metallic objects. Gareth obeyed and afterward stepped into the metal detector. That went off without a hitch. No surprise there. None of them had any weapons. He admitted he missed his gun, but he'd have to make do.

Gareth's comrades also cleared the checkpoint. Now they'd gained access to Nerboros. The machine they sought rested on the third floor, but their first goal was to contact Drebin. Ed waited for them in Lab Thirteen. There, the spy would provide them with useful items they couldn't smuggle inside by themselves.

The complex took the form of a massive labyrinth. Corridors branched off in every direction. Worse, the bland white walls and sterile décor offered few points of reference. They passed a rare water cooler or plant once in a while, but little else, which rendered navigation challenging. Since bringing a map had posed too much risk, Ed had provided oral instructions, but Gareth still let out a sigh of relief when he spotted a chart hanging on a wall. Careful to be discreet, he studied it from a distance, fearing the sentries might find it suspicious that a regular employee needed to consult a map. However, no one paid attention to him. That sent a tingle down his spine. With such a critical device here, security should have been increased. He told himself that was probably the case on the third floor. Besides, new employees must have been frequent enough, so he worried for nothing.

Thanks to the chart, Gareth and his group located Lab Thirteen five minutes later. The door required a valid ID card. Once again, Gareth swiped his. A loud alarm blared. He almost jumped out of surprise. Had Ed betrayed them? Intrigued by the noise, a nearby guard approached and Gareth's heartbeat raced.

"A problem, sir?" The man adopted a polite but firm tone.

Gareth scratched his head, fighting the urge to pounce. "I don't understand... we're supposed to have access. There must be a glitch in the system."

"I see." The guard frowned and rubbed his chin. "That happens sometimes. Come with me to the central office, please. We'll straighten this out."

That wouldn't do at all. They couldn't refuse, but if they complied, they'd be caught. Before he had a chance to think of an answer, Patricia said, "But it doesn't make sense. We were transferred here yesterday, and we opened the door just fine. This is Lab Fourteen, right?"

"No, it's Thirteen. Fourteen's over there." As Gareth resisted laughing, he prayed his abundant perspiration remained unnoticed. That Patricia, always so quick on her feet. Impressive, but she'd bought them a few minutes at best. Once they failed to open Lab Fourteen, the Ostarkiran would be even more skeptical. And their card wouldn't work for sure. Only a miracle would save them now.

Chapter 4

"James, I contacted you today because I believe I should at last reveal my identity," the Doctor said in his monotone voice.

As a response, James scoffed. "You already did. Aren't you the first human?"

"Oh, I am indeed." The president nodded. "However, do you not agree that is rather nonspecific? There are billions of humans on earth. Which one might I be?"

"If you say you're my father, I'll smash my minicomp," James warned without a hint of humor.

The smiley in the cyborg's electronic eye animated in a motion suggesting a roll of the eyes. "Oh, please. As if I would attempt such a pathetic old joke. Is it not evident that I am your mother?"

James crossed his arms. "Don't test me."

"Not even a single pity laugh? As you wish, I will be serious. I was a medical doctor in LA, a surgeon to be more precise, though I suppose that should not be surprising. I was considered a genius who showed great promise of a bright future in his field. While I fulfilled those expectations, it was not on earth. As far as home is concerned, I met a premature demise under mysterious circumstances. The police must have been so confused. From their point of view"—the cyborg snapped his fingers—"poof, I vanished without a trace. No doubt they failed to resolve the mystery, given I teleported to Nirnivia." Then he reached down, outside the camera's range. "This old mementos shall reveal my identity." He presented a warped plastic card with burned edges. Had that thing survived a fire? Despite the damage, the photo remained somewhat recognizable. It depicted a smiling blond and blue-eyed man. The visage brought James a shiver, but he was unsure why. Next to the picture, letters spelled out a name, but charred black spots obscured it. By squinting, James deciphered a few of them. M**ue* *hev**ie*.

That face... that letter pattern... my brain warned me I should recognize them, but my heart refused to listen. It didn't make sense. Did the Doctor really want me to believe he was him?
—Thoughts of James Hunter, Hocmar 28, 2134, on the Nirnivian calendar

With a flash of comprehension, James gasped and stepped backward, almost dropping the minicomp. "Um, but... no... you can't mean..."

The mechanical man leaned forward while linking his hands together. "Oh, but I most definitively do, James."

Chapter 5

While resisting a gulp, Gareth approached Lab Fourteen's door with his Nirnivian companions and the guard in tow. Various solutions rushed through his brain, moving so fast he lacked time to consider them. The ideas ranged from ludicrous—knock down the Ostarkiran, finish the mission through force—to realistic but unsatisfying—admit defeat, surrender. Sweat covered Gareth's skin. In particular, one annoying bead rolled down his neck, tickling him. What should he do? He aimed a discreet glance toward the others. By their blank expressions, they shared his hopelessness. Soon, the guard scowled and tilted his head in a manner suggesting suspicion. No more delay possible. As he forced himself to keep a straight face, Gareth lifted the ID card. A second before he scanned it, a voice echoed from behind.

"Hey, guys, there you are!" Happy for the distraction, yet still worried about what he'd do next, Gareth turned and faced the source. A bearded man with curly blond hair waved at them. Though they'd never met him, Gareth recognized him from the pictures his superiors had provided. Ed Drebin, their mole. The spy smiled at the Ostarkiran. "They're my new colleagues. I hope they didn't give you any trouble, buddy!"

The guard shrugged. "Not really, I think they're lost or something."

"Ah well, that happens all the time with new guys. This place's a maze and all the corridors look the same." A chuckle escaped Drebin's lips. "It's like they repeated the background to save money. Don't worry, I'll take care of them. Oh"—he snapped his fingers—"you're still joining us at the pub this weekend?"

"Sure thing! I better return to my rounds, I'll see you around."

"All right, have a nice day!" On that note, the sentry left and Gareth risked a sigh of relief. Once Ed judged the Ostarkiran out of range, he gestured for them to follow him back to Lab Thirteen.

"I'm very sorry," he whispered as he unlocked the door and they stepped inside. "I realized I messed up the IDs and went to find you. Thank Ulgorack I stumbled across you at the last minute."

Fermin glared at the mole and opened his mouth. No doubt he intended to deliver a scolding. With his hand, Gareth signaled him to hold his tongue. While Fermin swallowed his words, the grimace he settled for implied they tasted sour. Gareth wished to chastise Ed himself, but an argument might raise suspicion. Still, deep down he panicked. Forging the level one ID had posed a trivial challenge. Far bigger obstacles waited ahead, and they depended on Ed to get past them. Was the guy reliable? If they couldn't count on him, they were screwed. In the old war, Gareth had dealt with an incompetent colleague who'd ruined a mission and... *No, remember Dr. Crane's advice, focus on the present.*

"Just give me a minute." With that, Drebin headed for a nearby closet. Gareth used the opportunity to scan the room. It proved less than impressive. White walls like the rest of Nerboros so far, and no decorations. Two scientists typing on computers served as the lone occupants, save Gareth and his crew. The lack of a crowd must have been the reason the spy had chosen this spot.

"There you go," Ed murmured as he offered them a small briefcase. "Enjoy!"

Gareth already knew the package's contents. First, four pistols for emergencies. They'd rather not fight, but at least they'd be armed should the need arise. Next, the valise concealed communication devices so they could contact Drebin. The mole had spent the previous days planting backdoors in the research facility's computer system. From his personal minicomp, Ed could hack into the central unit and play amazing tricks. If they required help, they only had to call and ask. The whole scheme relied on those viruses. If the Ostarkirans discovered them, Gareth and his squad were done for, but that was unlikely. That left the most important item, new key cards granting access to the second and third floors. These had demanded extra effort to falsify and so Ed had finished them late, preventing him from sending them to HQ before the mission. Given he'd botched the straightforward level one passes, Gareth had difficulty trusting these more complex ones. Based on how Patricia shook her head and Yvan clenched his fist, not to mention Fermin's glare, his teammates shared his apprehension. That was bad.

Chapter 6

And that's how I learned Doctor Death was in fact Miguel, Rose's dearest husband. I didn't want to believe it. Really, I'm not sure why it bothered me so much, but just thinking about it sickened me.

—Thoughts of James Hunter, Hocmar 28, 2134, on the Nirnivian calendar

"No, no, no, no, that's impossible!" James gritted his teeth. "You can't be Miguel! There's no way!"

"James, your surprise is unwarranted. Do you not realize it is the only logical option?"

"That's not true! You could be Rose's brother! Laurence hates her and he disap—"

"Please, James, stop this drivel. That theory implies Laurence is human or has a good reason to pretend he is." The Doctor leaned forward. "Name one."

"Uhhh..."

The smiley in his electronic eye winked. "Then I suppose you see my point."

"But, no, it can't be... Miguel is dead!" James frowned. "He died in a raid; it's your fault! Ostarkiran soldiers killed him! Rose doesn't like talking about her husband, but she told me that much."

"That is partially true—the man Rose married is no more." Technical limitations ensured the president's tone stayed dull and emotionless. As for his facial expressions, his injuries rendered those limited and hard to read. Despite this, James sensed sadness in his posture. "Most of my body has been replaced by a machine. I assure you, nobody survives such a hell unscathed. My mind is forever scarred, changing me into a different person, which is why I forsook my name. However, in the strictest sense, Miguel Chevalier remains alive."

"Rose would never marry you! She hates you!"

The cyborg shrugged. "Does she? I do not believe so. In that case, she would not cry whenever I am mentioned. Our history is complicated. Rose preferred to hide the truth from you and acted in consequence."

"No, you're lying!"

"James, I know it is hard, but you must use your brain rather than your heart."

"My brain?" A nervous laugh escaped his lips. "My brain tells me it's bullshit! So you're the first human and Rose's husband? I'm not buying it. Why would she marry some guy from another universe? You're not even the same species!"

"An interesting argument." The mechanical man rubbed his speaker. "Alas, it is flawed. Rumor has it Janice Ricdeau has been—how shall I put it?— affectionate toward you."

A blush reddened James's cheeks. "It's not like that." He scratched the back of his head. "Janice helped me get used to Valardir. She's, uh, just a friend."

Or so I assumed, but I remembered that red dress Janice had worn when she'd invited me to the restaurant. That was... well, sexier than I'd expected. Could she have intended it as something more? But nah, there was no way, right?

—Thoughts of James Hunter, Hocmar 28, 2134, on the Nirnivian calendar

"If that is your take on it, I shall believe you, though my source is quite convinced of Ms. Ricdeau's affection toward you."

That gave me a shudder. I lived in a secure military complex and the Doctor had discovered that much information on me and Janice? How? More and more, I understood why everyone feared him. That guy was always one step ahead.

—Thoughts of James Hunter, Hocmar 28, 2134, on the Nirnivian calendar

"Regardless, it does not matter. Yes, humans and Gorumars are different species, but they share a similar DNA structure. During my tenure as a Nirnivian doctor, I studied their physiology in detail. Mostly, we are the same, though they possess a superior build quality. That is why, despite inferior living conditions compared to a first-world country on earth, their life expectancy is above ninety years old, and many reach above a hundred. Based on my research, even interbreeding should be possible. But I am rambling, forgive me. The important part is that, considering humans are basically Gorumars, marriage between a Nirnivian and an American is not so far-fetched. In Rose's case it is probable. Consider this, James. She is special: the holy Melkar. People put her on a pedestal and refuse to see the woman behind the icon. I am certain Rose mentioned how lonely she is as a result. Imagine how hard it would be for her to find love when simple friendship eludes her grasp. No Nirnivian man would entertain romantic feelings for the Voice of God, and if I am wrong and it happened, he would not dare pursue it. The only exceptions are ambitious types who would court her for prestige. Rose would reject those suitors. However, for a human, Melkar is an insignificant title. It is a mere word devoid of meaning. Therefore, I saw beyond the legend."

That made more sense than I wished to admit. Rose had confided she'd never dated before Miguel. He was the first who hadn't cared if she was the Melkar; it had meant nothing

to him. To be frank, I haven't met a Nirnivian like that. Some don't believe Rose is a prophet, but they don't see the real her. Rather, they often hate her for what she represents, like the Timanites, or Jonathan. Doctor Death gave me something to ponder, but I wasn't convinced yet and he noticed that.

—Thoughts of James Hunter, Hocmar 28, 2134, on the Nirnivian calendar

"You still distrust me, but I have more facts for you to consider. Have you ever seen Rose's wedding ring?"

James crossed his arms. "Sure, she showed it to me."

"Have you discerned anything peculiar?"

In his mind, James visualized the ornament. While his memory proved lacking, he remembered a standard ring, other than the size of the stone adorning it. That jewel must've cost a fortune. "No, it seemed normal. It was on the correct finger and everything."

The mechanical man nodded. "Yes, the ring is normal, but there is still something strange." James scowled, but he stayed silent. "Fine, I shall guide you. I feel that Daniel's ring is a bit too plain, do you agree?"

Then it struck me. Daniel didn't wear a ring; neither did Madeleine, nor Jonathan. That's when I understood that maybe Nirnivians didn't exchange rings during their marriage ceremony. Why would they? It's not like every culture on earth did, so why would beings from another universe?

—Thoughts of James Hunter, Hocmar 28, 2134, on the Nirnivian calendar

"Indeed, Rose is the only Nirnivian with a wedding ring. She got the idea from me. When I explained how my people trade rings symbolizing their endless union, she liked it and suggested we do the same. As an atheist, I do not care for futile rituals; however, she insisted, so I agreed. In fact, I still wear mine too."

James scoffed. "That's nice, but you'll have to do better than that."

"I shall comply. Have you noticed how everyone hates me with a passion, but Rose does not display the same level of hostility?"

A shrug came from James. "Can't say I have. She hardly talks about you."

"No matter, plenty of arguments remain. Have you seen pictures of Miguel?" James nodded. "Excellent. I've changed significantly; however, what I consider my finest feature remains recognizable."

The only remaining part of his original body was his face, so I studied it. He was grotesque. I tried to remember Miguel's photo. It wasn't easy. Rose had married a handsome man. The Doctor looked nothing like him. Then again, he was so disfigured he didn't look like anyone. Still searching for the answer, I gazed into his lone organic eye. That beautiful deep blue eye, just like those Miguel had. I gasped at the realization.

—Thoughts of James Hunter, Hocmar 28, 2134, on the Nirnivian calendar

"Okay, yes... you..." James sighed. "Um, I can't be one hundred percent sure, but I give up."

"A wise decision, my friend, for we mere mortals cannot ever be one hundred percent sure of anything. James, Rose is fond of you, but that does not mean you are safe. She used to love me a lot more, and that did not stop her from delivering me to a fate worse than death itself."

Chapter 7

Gareth and the others stood in line for the elevator that would bring them to the second level. While their destination waited on the third floor, this lift lacked the capability to take them that far. Still, they had to start somewhere. When they arrived, the guards fired a suspicious glare at them. Gareth's muscles tensed. New faces must have proved rare, and thus their presence fueled suspicion. While he resisted a hard swallow, he reached for his ID card and handed it over. If Ed messed up again... but, no, the scanning machine emitted a success jingle as a green light flashed, and Gareth almost exhaled in relief. His three companions also passed the test without a hitch.

Soon, the elevator doors closed behind them and they started their ascent. Nobody else rode along, which gave them a moment to relax. Not for long, however. About midway through the trip, the earpiece Drebin had provided Gareth vibrated, and Gareth accepted the call.

"Hey, this is Ed. I, uh, made a mistake when I entered your fake profiles. You won't have access to the third floor. Don't worry, the cards are fine, so I can fix it. Just wait on the second floor until I contact you again."

The transmission cut off before Gareth could answer. It seemed the spy had realized he deserved a tongue lashing and declined to offer the opportunity. What a fool! This would end in tragedy, like when that idiot Roger had screwed them in the battle of...

No, that was neither here nor there. *Relax*. After calming down, Gareth relayed the news to the others.

Disappointed groans echoed. Fermin punctuated the sound by shaking his head, while Patricia preferred a face palm.

"The giant douche will get us all killed!" a fist-clenching Yvan whispered.

Though Gareth shared his anger, he remained focused. "Relax. Drebin noticed before it was too late. That's the important thing."

"Is it?" Fermin gritted his teeth. "What are we supposed to do? Walk around and enjoy the scenery? That's dangerous. The more we wait, the more we stand out."

"Besides, he messed up the level one cards, and now this." Patricia crossed her arms. "We can't trust him."

Truth be told, Gareth felt the same, but he wanted them to concentrate on the mission. Drebin was a liability, but they needed him. They could only pray they'd succeed despite his flaws.

"Guys, I don't like this either, but give Ed some credit. Yes, it's been messy, but he got us this far. He's doing the best he can, like us." The others mumbled that he was right, but Gareth doubted he'd convinced them. He couldn't blame them, though, since his own words left him cold.

Before long, the ride ended. In appearance, this floor shared the previous one's visual styling, yet the atmosphere proved oppressive. Extra sentries patrolled the area, and Gareth spotted several cameras. Not only that, but the guards showed more alertness and their glares suggested they might jump you and bust your skull at any moment.

The four of them progressed at a slow pace and talked among themselves. The conversation lacked meaning. Instead, they indulged in irrelevant technobabble to pass for scientists. Gareth prayed the surrounding Ostarkirans didn't listen too closely. Regardless of Ed's warning, they headed for the next elevator in the hope he'd contact them before they reached it, but the lift came into view with no word from Drebin. At the last second, Gareth gestured toward another hallway veering to the right. The others obeyed his signal, and they turned.

For fifteen minutes, Gareth and his group marched along unknown passages without a destination. Each turn they took, Gareth committed to memory. After all, they'd have to retrace their steps later. The trip went fine until a guard frowned while looking at them. She tapped her chin and, without delay, advanced toward them as her scowl intensified. Beads of sweat covered Gareth's brow. This was just like that botched infiltration in... never mind that. He presented his palm to the others so they'd stop. Any attempt to retreat would raise suspicion. A lone solution offered itself—facing the sentry's questions and bluffing. Gareth braced himself and straightened as the guard crossed his path and kept walking. His mouth gaped. Whatever had drawn her attention was behind him. Though curious, he declined to peek at whatever that might've been.

About thirty seconds later, Drebin contacted them again and claimed he'd solved the problem. A churning in Gareth's stomach confirmed he remained skeptical. Still, he figured they'd better return to the elevator. Somehow, he remembered the way, but he spotted an Ostarkiran following them. Unsure what to do, Gareth continued as if nothing had happened. Should they diverge from the sure path to fool the guy and lose him? A fair strategy, but this being a maze, they might get lost. When the guard spun into a different corridor, Gareth took a deep breath. It had been a coincidence.

They arrived at the elevator and again their ID cards got the job done. Once inside, they ascended toward the third and final level. The target stood within reach, but they couldn't rest yet. Gareth swallowed hard as he visualized the next step. As if to voice his disgust, Patricia moaned and said, "So I guess we have to..." She cringed. "Oh God, I don't want to think about it."

"It'll be okay, we've been through worse."

"Maybe, but damn it, not by much." Everyone nodded in agreement. Then the door opened.

Chapter 8

"While a cliché, it is true, James," the Doctor said. "I remember meeting Rose like it was yesterday. I have never believed in God. From a young age, I concluded that none of the religions made sense and embraced atheism. When I met Rose, that was the only occasion on which I considered the possibility that I had been mistaken. There stood an angel, and if angels existed, so did God."

His voice was as monotonous as ever, and his face remained emotionless. Miguel couldn't help it since his body wouldn't allow otherwise. Yet, despite those limitations, I felt his nostalgia. It was strange: Doctor Death had denounced Rose and warned me she was dangerous, but he spoke of her with so much passion, I wouldn't have been surprised if he had still been in love with her.

—Thoughts of James Hunter, Hocmar 28, 2134, on the Nirnivian calendar

"The wings played a part in the illusion, but it went beyond that. She conveyed such grace it seemed impossible for her to be a mortal being of flesh and blood. Rose's beauty transcended physicality. I have dated several gorgeous women, some with features so perfect they put Rose's to shame, and yet they paled when compared to her magnificence. It was like her inner self shone through her appearance. As for Rose's voice, it was magical: a sweet melody no bird could match even if they hummed for a million years. No wonder the masses are enchanted by her mere words. Once, I convinced Rose to sing for me, James.

That was marvelous—a delight as I never dared imagine. How unfortunate she is so shy she does not dare perform in public. If you ever have the chance to hear her songs, I urge you to indulge. But I digress. The point is: when I saw Rose, I knew she had to be a divine being sent by God to show me the error of my ways."

I understood what Miguel meant since I had a similar experience when I met Rose. She had a powerful presence that made it obvious she was more than the naked eye could see.

—Thoughts of James Hunter, Hocmar 28, 2134, on the Nirnivian calendar

"And yet she was not an angel." The president shrugged. "In fact, Rose did not know what angels were. Regardless of semantics, I was convinced she was special." The mechanical man paused for a moment as he lowered his neck. "Tell me, do you believe in love at first sight?"

The question caused James to frown. "No, I don't. Uh, when someone tells me they fell in love at first sight, I say they're a victim of lust at first sight."

"Is that so? Then it seems we agree. True love cannot be achieved in a fraction of a second. To deeply care for another, you must explore their inner self. And once obtained, love requires constant maintenance to sustain. It is a fragile treasure and will fade away should you leave it unattended. I have believed so for my entire life; however, with Rose, it was the closest a man can come to love at first sight. In other, less eloquent, terms: I had a raging case of lust at first sight. I do not delude myself; it was not mutual. Oh, as a visitor from a parallel universe, I intrigued Rose, but I was a mere curiosity. Still, I conquered her heart. I must hurry, so I shall gloss over the details. Suffice it to say it was an arduous battle. I prevailed, and she became my wife. The years we spent together were pure bliss. No relationship is perfect, and we had our share of problems, but damn it, James, we made it work better than most. If you will accept an additional piece of cheese, I felt like the luckiest man alive. I called her my love, my joy, my skeptical angel."

"Your skeptical angel?" James repeated while tilting his head. "What's that supposed to mean?"

"Originally, Rose reacted the same way. The angel part should be clear: she looks like one. As for skeptical, well, that is trickier. It refers to the fact that people here believe she is the Melkar and yet she does not. When it comes to her holy heritage, Rose is a skeptic. In a way, she is similar to an angel who denies she is a divine being. Hence, she was my skeptical angel."

His skeptical angel... yeah, I guess it's kinda clever... in a lame way.

—Thoughts of James Hunter, Hocmar 28, 2134, on the Nirnivian calendar

"I remember when Alcharia afflicted Rose. The mere thought that she might die was unbearable. I would have done anything to be the one crippled in bed instead. That would have been much more acceptable. There was nothing I could do except stay at her side and remain strong. I even prayed—a delusion I'd always declined to indulge in. As you know, she survived. When she woke, it was the second happiest day of my life, the first being when we wed. The future we were almost denied was given back, promising to be grandiose. Unfortunately, I can be wrong on occasion. Everything ends, including true love. The blissful future became a nightmare. For the years of devotion I provided, my recompense ended up been transformed into this broken shell of my former self."

Before that, I never fully grasped that deep down, Doctor Death was a living being filled with the same feelings as everyone else. He lost smiles and frowns, laughter and tears. His face was mutilated, his mouth gone. Even his voice had been taken away. Miguel was more machine than flesh. For the first time, I realized how wrong I had been. He was a human. Even if he lied about being from earth, he was a human in the same way the Gorumars were. I'm ashamed to admit it, but his appearance was the main reason I didn't want to trust the guy. Miguel was so passionate then. With his only eye, he showed me a greater range of emotions than most did with their whole body. While I couldn't figure out if he told the entire truth, I was sure that he had been in love with Rose in the past and might still be.

—Thoughts of James Hunter, Hocmar 28, 2134, on the Nirnivian calendar

"The craziest part, James, is that despite the torture I endured, I have no regrets. Those years we shared were pure ecstasy. Perhaps a slice of heaven is worth an eternity in hell. If I were given the opportunity to relive the past, I have no idea what I would do. One might assume that I would stay away from Rose as if she were the devil. Maybe I would do so, and yet I cannot be certain. There is a possibility I would run to Rose and start it all over again. Her mere presence is intoxicating. I miss her so much. James, if knowing her madness, you remained by her side until she destroys you, I would understand. Rose clouds the mind like nothing else and introduces a yearning greater than any drug. However, you should be aware of the facts so that, should you make a foolish decision, it will at least be an informed one."

Chapter 9

Disgusting served as the best word to describe Gareth's current situation. If he had realized enlisting in NISDA implied ending up knee-deep in viscous gunk filling a trash compartment, he might have declined. Based on the others' grimacing expressions, he expected they shared his opinion. The dark goop stained their clothes and hampered their movements because of its consistency. Worst of all, the stench proved unbearable. Like a garbage dump, but far more potent. With every breath, Gareth gagged, and Yvan had vomited earlier. Should this experience continue long enough, they'd follow his lead eventually. At least no similar event had occurred during the last war, so his memory spared him a panic attack. That was the lone positive.

Despite their protests, Ed assured them this was the only way. The machine they targeted waited in a room teeming with researchers. They could not destroy it while surrounded by witnesses, at least not if they wished to escape afterward. The area needed to be emptied. They lacked the firepower to kill everyone and so required a less drastic option. Drebin was once again the key. Nerboros's laboratories could be dangerous. Sometimes, disasters happened. The spy would trigger an alarm signaling an event so catastrophic the whole level would be evacuated. From there, accomplishing their mission became a simple matter, provided they acted fast. However, this plan posed a problem. It'd be suspicious to have four scientists running in the wrong direction. Because of this, Drebin decided they should hide somewhere no one would see them: this huge garbage compactor they now inhabited.

"Ugh, this smell." Patricia covered her mouth with her palm and retched. "I'm going to be sick."

"Hold on; it won't be long." Though Gareth doubted he spoke the truth, he assumed that was what she'd rather hear.

Patricia nodded when a high-pitched squeal echoed. Then a furry shape smeared with filth scurried between her legs, grazing her. A rittle—a small rodent that lived in the sewer, and a notorious disease carrier. As Patricia glimpsed the animal, she threw up. The others averted their gaze lest they suffer the same fate. Two out of four now. Ah well, at least the revolting creature didn't bite her.

"Oh dear Ulgorack," she mumbled while shaking her head. "I hate rittles."

Yvan chuckled. "Then you're in the wrong place. Lots of rittles here—junk's candy to them. Believe me, there's much worse."

"Please, don't!" Patricia lifted her hand as if it might shield her from Yvan's words.

"They say there are weird mutant creatures living in these trash compartments. The kind with tentacles that grab you and pull you in deep where you can't breathe and you die of suffocation. Then they eat you."

A sob came from Patricia. "Stop, please! Just stop!"

Gareth fired a glare at Yvan, but he continued. "If there are some of those here, we're screwed. They're hard to kill. Death by drowning in trash... that doesn't sound fun."

"Shut up!"

"I agree, shut up," Gareth said while pointing a menacing finger. "You're not helping, Yvan. It's an urban legend. Those things don't exist."

Silence settled in for a little while, but it wasn't meant to be, given that Fermin broke it moments later.

"I hate it here! It's so small." A cough escaped his lips. "I can't breathe." Gareth knew the big man suffered from slight claustrophobia. "This place compresses the trash on a daily schedule." Fermin's voice trembled. "Any minute now, the walls will close in and crush us with this freaking garbage—"

"Don't start, Fermin. We're safe. Ed shut down the system."

He laughed. "Yeah, and Ed is an incompetent who almost got us killed twice already."

"Enough, keep your cool." To be honest, Gareth worried too. Not about monsters or the walls, but his own comrades. The unreliability displayed by Drebin combined with the nightmarish location fueled their imagination. Sometimes a soldier's own mind can become their deadliest enemy. He wondered if that would prove true for his own. Was he really ready for this? In silence, Gareth prayed the alarm would go off so they could leave this godforsaken dump. As if to answer his call, a deafening siren resounded. Ed's deception had begun. Around fifteen minutes more and they'd begin the mission for real.

Chapter 10

As the Doctor finished his last sentence, James frowned. "You're always yapping about how Rose's dangerous, but you never told me why. Rose's one of the nicest, most compassionate women I've ever met. She cares about people. Can't say she strikes me as the evil type."

The cyborg nodded. "On the surface, she does not seem to be. However, should you investigate further—well, to be frank, you will reach the same conclusion. I would not characterize Rose as evil. You see, James, she believes she acts in Nirnivia's best interests. Rose does care about her people and toils to better their lives, but she is misguided. While Rose's intentions are pure, her methods are flawed. She became a tyrant, but not out of greed or self-interest. In the name of the greater good, Rose and those close to her will soon unleash a catastrophe of unequaled proportion. If allowed to continue, the poor fools will destroy everything they hold dear to preserve it." Miguel lowered his head as the smile vanished from the emoticon displayed inside his electronic eye. "Rose deserves blame, but she is a victim of her own existence. James, you cannot imagine the pressure she carries on her shoulders or the pain she has endured. Her not killing herself is a testimony to Rose's strength. Unfortunately, her torments have left her devastated and even insane, though she hides it well, to the point that you can interact with Rose for years without noticing. I am skilled at psychology, yet I was married to the woman, shared a house, and I only realized far too late."

As much as I wished to deny it, I already knew Rose was broken emotionally. Her mask smiled and laughed, but inside she suffered. A single look into her eyes revealed it. Even when Rose was happy, an aura of sadness remained. As for insanity—talking with her mirror counted as a sign, I guess. Hell, she'd once warned me that maybe she did it because she'd lost her mind.

—Thoughts of James Hunter, Hocmar 28, 2134, on the Nirnivian calendar

"Um, yeah, I know what you mean. Rose mentioned her past."

The president shook his head. "No, you have no idea. I am certain what she revealed barely scratches the surface. Rose lived a miserable life. Despite what she did to me, I pity her. However, no matter how tragic and benevolent the villain is, the hero must save the world." Again, Miguel shook his head. "No, my analogy is flawed. I have committed atrocities and became a villain myself. In this war, there is no one righteous. I regret my transgressions. I could not find an alternative. That is not an excuse but a failing, and I do not expect nor deserve forgiveness for my sins."

"You still haven't told me what's going on."

"Even I am not aware of everything, but what I discovered is appalling. It involves Project Ekelon, NISDA's dirty little secret. Ekelon can manipulate information and censor unpleasant truths to make the military's rule supreme. The worst part is, the Council is unaware of its existence. Daniel Ricdeau is running an illegal operation that grants him command over Nirnivia from the shadows. Since I do not wish to trouble your sleep, I will stop there."

Project Ekelon... the mechanical freak had mentioned it before, but he wasn't clear. His new explanation didn't help. Jonathan had once told me conspiracy theorists thought Ekelon was a social control system. That fit with the Doctor's claim, but Jonathan had assured me it was a fantasy: the required tech didn't exist. Was there something he was unaware of, or was Miguel feeding me bullshit?

—Thoughts of James Hunter, Hocmar 28, 2134, on the Nirnivian calendar

"That sounds bad, but Rose wouldn't... are you sure she's involved?"

"Perhaps she is not, but I possess evidence suggesting otherwise. When I discovered the truth behind Ekelon, I tried telling Rose. For my efforts, she attempted to reward me with a bullet. She missed"—the cyborg pointed toward his torso—"but the encounter triggered a series of events that resulted in this broken body. That is why I am convinced my dearest angel is aware of her father's transgressions. Most Nirnivians follow Rose with blind faith; however, she realizes such devotion can be crushed. If I had exposed Ekelon, her disciples would have rebelled. How I survived is a miracle, and if I revealed the details, you would assume I was joking. It is an entertaining tale, but alas, there are more pressing concerns." Miguel paused for a second. "James, I am beyond certain Rose loved me. She cared for me more than for herself. In the end, her allegiance to Daniel proved stronger than love. Rose never forgave herself for what happened, but I have no doubt she would do it again. As the president of Ostark, I have sought to expose her. Sadly, I concluded that the only proof the Nirnivians will accept is a genuine confession from the holy prophet. Thus my kidnapping attempts. I hope that, by confining Rose, I can reason with her. Perhaps my efforts are destined to fail, but I shall try. In the meantime, I am seeking alternative solutions, but so far they have been fruitless. James, I swear that I will not hurt Rose. She has suffered enough." Another silence followed. "I must leave you soon, but there is one last detail to discuss before I go. Rose and the others have hidden a crucial fact from you— much more important than my identity."

James frowned. "What fact?"

The Doctor leaned forward. "That our home is entirely within our grasp."

Chapter 11

Gareth and his squad reached their destination at last. With the level emptied, they found the correct laboratory, and now they stared at the machine they sought. The size dwarfed Gareth. He'd heard of its vast dimensions beforehand, but somehow that hadn't conveyed the sense of scale. Thank God they only needed a tiny part. The rest, they aimed to destroy.

From a distance, Gareth studied the device in awe. In the middle stood a large rectangular metallic frame resembling a giant doorway so huge a grown man could walk through it. A staircase led to its base, giving the impression that stepping inside was the intent. Complex electronics beyond their comprehension surrounded the apparent gate.

At any rate, they had to hurry. Gareth and Patricia headed toward the machine while Yvan and Fermin guarded the area. Once close enough, Gareth reached for an explosive charge Ed Drebin had provided in the package he'd given them earlier. Then he fixed it on the device and grabbed another one. As for Patricia, she searched for the single piece they wanted. By the time Gareth had set five bombs, she called him.

"Gareth, come here, please. I don't like this." With a sick sensation in his stomach, he obeyed. Patricia held a small blue crystal that shimmered in the light. The smooth surface reflected his image.

"What's wrong?"

"Look." She turned the crystal, and now a crack ran down Gareth's mirrored face. "It's broken."

"What?" A frown formed on Gareth's brow as he realized their assignment proved futile. They'd risked their lives for nothing. Then, slowly, he grasped the implications and grimaced. "You don't think this is a trap, do you?"

Patricia frowned. "I've considered the possibility." The same held true for Gareth, but that made little sense. The device was real. Sure, it didn't work anymore, but it had before. Maybe when it had broken, Doctor Death had decided to use it as bait—but why? To capture a few Nirnivians? That hardly seemed worthwhile. Plus, if that was the plan, why wait so long before snatching them? The Ostarkirans could have imprisoned Gareth and his friends at the entrance if they'd desired. Gareth told himself that it couldn't be a trap. The machine failing had been a coincidence. While he kept repeating this in his mind, his bad presentiments remained.

As if to confirm his doubts, a legion of WarBots rolled into the area, guns firing. Fermin and Yvan shot them, but the robots' armor was too resistant for their bullets. Soon, the WarBots' superior firepower reduced the two soldiers to organic mush. An intense sweat covered Gareth. The red shirt he wore under the scientist coat suddenly felt far too warm.

As the WarBots scanned the area for the remaining targets, Gareth concealed himself behind the machine and grabbed the transmitter Drebin had offered him earlier. Besides communicating with the spy, it allowed text messages to be sent back to Valardir through BBR's communication's array. As fast as his fingers could manage, Gareth typed a short note and hit the send button. This task completed, he seized the detonator for the explosives he'd set up moments ago. He glanced at Patricia and she nodded. A strange calm filled Gareth. Perhaps Janice had been correct and he had been seeking a place to die. With one last prayer and a wish that in the eyes of Ulgorack and Timagoron, this didn't count as suicide, he pressed the switch.

Chapter 12

Sitting on the opposite side of the desk, Ron watched Daniel talk on the phone. With every passing moment, the Commander's frown intensified. By the end of the conversation, his lips twitched. "Yes, I understand. Thank you, Nicky." Daniel hung up and sighed before rubbing his brow as if assailed by a headache. Curious, Ron leaned forward. Daniel joined his hands in a pyramid and stared at him. "Gareth sent us an update about the mission. Two words, 'Crystal cracked.'"

A second passed before Ron realized the implication and scowled. "What the freak?"

"I'm confused too, but at least the device is destroyed even if it wasn't our doing."

"Yeah, but what shitty timing." A scowl formed on Tigh's brow. "You think Doctor Death's screwing with us? Like it's some sort of trap?"

Daniel shrugged. "Maybe. He's a tricky one, but we shouldn't overestimate him. Refined Yomorok crystals are fragile. They break down easily—that's why they're rare. That expert must have used the teleporter a lot, straining the crystal, and it shattered."

"Sure, but it's freaking strange. The goddamn thing broke when we sent a squad to destroy it. What are the chances? I don't like it." A groan escaped Ron's lips. "What if the machine went kaput a while back and that bastard Doctor Death used it as bait?"

"Oh, I see." Daniel tapped his cheek with his index finger. "The teleporter became useless, so he moved it to

Nerboros to lure us. Since that's a third-rate facility with lacking security, we took a chance and fell for it."

Ron snapped his fingers in confirmation. "Sounds crazy as balls, but with that son of a bitch it's possible."

"Yes, it matches his theatrical flair." Daniel grunted. "The problem is the motive. He has nothing to gain except killing or capturing a few of our soldiers. Why bother?"

After an exhale, Tigh scratched behind his head. "I don't know, I freaking don't, but I'm telling you I smell bullshit." He paused, grimaced. "Dan, listen, if Doctor Death pulled something like this, it means I'm right and there's—"

"Yes, I know, a traitor in Valardir," the Commander finished for him. That threat was one they'd considered before. While Daniel had recognized the possibility, he'd rejected it. Ron, however, had insisted it was the case. Several recent incidents had suggested a mole, such as the way Doctor Death had contacted James. Though the method used had involved an emitter installed outside their complex, so that didn't mean much. Then the Ostarkirans had discovered the Orontian launchpad. The assassination attempt on the president had also failed. Still, none of these guaranteed a traitor's presence.

Except for James, no new faces had joined Valardir for two years. Thus, if their enemies had an informant, someone they trusted had betrayed NISDA. They studied the possibilities and concluded that if a traitor existed, they weren't capable of kidnapping Rose, since they'd never attempted to. This implied the spy lacked access to Valardir, or didn't have the physical prowess and training to orchestrate such a daring abduction.

Daniel shook his head. "But it's a stretch. For all we knew, the crystal cracked earlier today and the WarBots were deployed because of our false alarm." A groan escaped Daniel's lips. "Besides, this changes nothing. Even if there is a mole, that doesn't mean he's in Valardir. Councillors and officers from different facilities knew the details of the relevant operations."

"Dan, we have to step things up. This is freaking serious."

"Yes, but don't be too quick to judge. Everyone here earned our trust. We can't let this degenerate into a witch hunt. That'd be doing the Doctor a favor," Daniel moaned as he dismissed the conversation with a wave. "Anyway, the briefing starts in five minutes. Let's go to the war room."

"Fine, whatever." Ron waggled a lecturing finger. "But we'll pick this up again after we're done."

"Sure, Ron." On that note, Daniel stood up and stepped away, only to stop in his tracks. "Oh, wait a minute." He reached for his phone and unhooked it from its base, rendering it wireless. "I promised Rose I'd call as soon as I had news. I'll do it while we walk there."

Ron resisted a groan. As during the hostage situation, Rose had stuck her nose where it didn't belong. This mission resonated with her on a personal level. She abused her privilege of being a councillor and Daniel's daughter to meddle. At least it wasn't to a ridiculous extent, like with that Onel business. Still, Tigh decided he'd have a talk with his old friend and colleague later.

***

Home. I had been stuck in this universe for several months; going home already felt impossible. Still, I desperately wanted to. It was my life. I'd never thought much of my life since it seemed pointless, and I'd accomplished nothing noteworthy. Once I lost it, it became way more important and special. Now

Doctor Death dangled earth before my eyes. I wanted it so badly I could taste it, but I didn't dare believe.

—Thoughts of James Hunter, Hocmar 28, 2134, on the Nirnivian calendar

Miguel tilted his head. "I see you remain doubtful, James. While I understand your reluctance, I assure you I am telling the truth. I have in my possession a device that can send you back. For our purposes, let us call it a multi-verse teleporter."

"So you built that machine for me?" James scoffed. "Gee, thanks, but that's hard to swallow."

To James's surprise, the president shook his head. "While I wish to help, James, I am far too busy. Multiverse teleporters are ancient and complex. The art of building them is forgotten. Functioning ones are rare, but I own three in working order."

My senses warned me it was a trick. The cyborg would lure me out and capture me. Then he'd use me as a bargaining chip. Hey, I'm not smart, but I'm not that stupid either.

—Thoughts of James Hunter, Hocmar 28, 2134, on the Nirnivian calendar

"Great! I guess I'll go to Ostark and you'll send me home right away."

The emoticon in the mechanical man's eyes grew somber. "I am afraid it is not so simple. First, I must locate earth. Picture a map. Each area is denoted by coordinates: longitude and latitude. The teleporter represents universes with coordinates also, except composed not of two numbers but thousands. To reach home, I require the correct sequence and have been searching for it since your arrival." Then Miguel closed his fist, and the emoji returned to its former happy self. "I am getting close, James. A couple months and it will be done. If you crave a change of scenery, you are welcome in Ostark, but I expect you are not ready for that leap of faith. No matter—for the short term, you are safe in Nirnivia. Rose will not harm you unless provoked. After all, you are her best friend." He paused. "There is one last thing, James. It is... unpleasant. Please, remember that I am only the messenger and that you should save your anger for the guilty party." Again, the president hesitated. "I am not the only one who possesses a multiverse teleporter. Nirnivia has one too. Rose hid that fact because she does not want you to leave. From Rose's warped perspective, you are now her only friend. She refuses to lose you and will thwart your every attempt to return, regardless of the cost."

That sounded ridiculous. Such an obvious lie. Rose wouldn't do that. Yeah, she had her issues, and sure, it'd be difficult for her. It's not like it'd be easy for me. I had met good people here, Rose included.

—Thoughts of James Hunter, Hocmar 28, 2134, on the Nirnivian calendar

While gritting his teeth, James crossed his arms. "No, you're wrong! Or just plain lying! Rose wouldn't do that!"

"Ah, but would I present such an outrageous claim without proof?" Miguel tapped his index finger against his speaker. "Actually, I have not mentioned this before because I lacked definitive evidence until today. It is more terrible than I have implied. Rose uses the Nirnivian military for her own selfish desires. NISDA is trying to destroy my multiverse teleporters so you can never find your way home."

Just thinking Rose could do that broke my heart. It was so cold—so cruel. I chased the feeling away, Rose had done nothing. The bastard was lying. He had to be. Then my minicomp's

screen started playing a video of people messing around with a large machine. The Doctor explained they were Nirnivian spies setting up explosive charges.

—Thoughts of James Hunter, Hocmar 28, 2134, on the Nirnivian calendar

"Stop! I'm not falling for it! This could be a fake!"

"I have been thoroughly honest with you, James, yet you still distrust me. It seems we are both doubting Thomases. So be it. It is likely that Rose is talking on the phone with her father about this very subject. How about we listen? If we are lucky, they might confirm I spoke the truth." The cyborg moved his arm. Though his hand went off screen, James deduced he pressed a button. Then a female voice echoed through the minicomp's speakers.

"Wait... we did all this for nothing? We sacrificed those soldiers for no reason? Like with Brucie?"

"Yes, I'm afraid so, princess."

"Dear God, it sounds like one of his mind games."

"Now, princess, this is important—you can't talk to James about this."

"Oh, Dad, you don't have to worry." The prophet sighed. "If Hunter ever learns that we tried to destroy a machine that could send him home, I doubt he'd take it well. It's best if he doesn't know."

Daniel's voice then said, "Good. Listen, princess, I have to go."

"All right, Dad."

No question that was Rose's voice. A cold sweat covered me. I couldn't deny Rose had said those words, no matter how much I wanted to. At first, I was stunned and couldn't react, so I sat there staring at the minicomp with my mouth gaping like an idiot. Then wave after wave of emotions drowned me:

rage, confusion, sadness, fear. Rose had fooled me—betrayed me. I'd believed she cared about me. How stupid I had been. And she'd dared call me her best friend. Loneliness had always been a problem in this universe; with horror, I understood how truly alone I was. I had precious few friends here. When Brucie had died, I'd lost one, and now with this revelation, I had none. Everyone plotted behind my back. While Miguel had opened my eyes, for all I knew he was using me for his own devices too. Could it be a fake, like the video? Maybe, but nobody had a voice like Rose, and somehow I doubted it could be replicated even by the most advanced technology.

—Thoughts of James Hunter, Hocmar 28, 2134, on the Nirnivian calendar

In shock, James yelled, "What the hell?"

"Hunter?" With a gasp, James dropped the minicomp, but not before he saw Miguel grasp his head with both hands. Had she heard him?

"James, no, do not talk. I forgot to warn you. Listen, I will help—"

Gray haze covered the screen before it returned to the game James had played earlier. He hopped to his feet and started pacing. If Rose had heard him, then... oh crap. What should he do?

No chance to answer that question—the doorbell rang, and soon Rose said through the interphone, "Hunter, what's going on?"

Episode 15

Choices

Chapter 1

Valar 13, 2134, on the Nirnivian calendar

"Hunter, what's going on?"

An intense fear seized James, squeezing his chest. His lungs refused to breathe. Should he let Rose in? Pretend he wasn't there? Even if he chose the former, the shock froze him in place. That bastard Miguel had never said that Rose would hear if he spoke. The mechanical man had warned James that she had to remain oblivious to their discussions, only to mess up like this? Worse, this had happened when the cyborg had revealed that Rose and the others were concealing the existence of a machine capable of sending him home. Now it seemed probable that Rose realized James's forbidden knowledge. According to Miguel, discovering Ekelon had brought about his current physical condition. What fate awaited James given that the president had shared the information with him? Whatever it might be, he had to figure something out.

What to do? James stood in a sealed chamber equipped with a single door. A person he needed to avoid waited behind that lone exit. The room lacked any other escape route. Besides, James lived in a high-security military complex filled with soldiers. Even if he managed a miracle, once outside, he'd have nowhere to go. James prayed for a solution and racked his brain for one, but his mind only responded with sentences declaring how screwed he was. Then the door slid open, revealing Rose in her white dress.

James swallowed hard. Though his body yearned to recoil, his muscles denied movement.

The alleged prophet stepped forward. "Hunter, it's weird. I was talking to Dad, and right after he hung up, I heard you through my phone." Rose paused and fixated on James for a moment. "Hunter, you're as white as a sheet. Are you feeling sick?"

"Um, I..." From there, his lips refused to budge. James doubted any words could save him anyway.

A scowl formed on Rose's brow. After a second of contemplation, she gasped and rested her palm on her heart. "Dear Ulgorack, it was you. That's why you're so terrified. But how?" Rose's eyes widened, and she held her head with both hands. "Oh, no. No, no, no, no, no. It was him! Somehow, he contacted you again, and you spoke to him. Please tell me I'm wrong."

It's funny, I was so scared of Rose learning the truth, but now that she had, a weight had been lifted from my shoulders. No need to stress about it anymore. That's how humans are. We worry and worry about the future, but once it happens, there's no point in doing that, is there? A sense of peace filled me, but soon it transformed into pure rage. That woman had lied to me. Manipulated me. Used me as a pet, like the Doctor claimed. She'd taken me for a fool and I'd proven her right. I remembered all we had gone through together. The laughs we'd enjoyed. The tears we'd shed. The Kuhard games I'd lost. I thought I was angry, but remembering—well, that made me furious. Sure, I'd die, but I intended to get everything off my chest before then.

—Thoughts of James Hunter, Hocmar 28, 2134, on the Nirnivian calendar

James glared at Rose and gritted his teeth. "You mean Miguel?" Rose's mouth gaped and her skin whitened to a shade almost rivaling his own. "Yeah, I talked to him. And, yes, I heard." The volume of his voice doubled without his intending it to. "I heard how you destroyed a machine that could send me back home! What the hell, Rose, why didn't you tell me?"

"Hunter, I'm sorry."

"Oh really? Are you sorry for Miguel too? He told me you shot him."

Rose's eyes watered, but she turned her head, blocking James's view. Instead of answering, the prophet dashed to the corridor. Before the door closed, she glanced at the guard. "Keep Hunter safe, but don't let him outside, no matter wh—" The shutting door cut off the rest of the sentence.

The rage gave me courage, but with Rose gone, it disappeared along with the effects of adrenaline. What now? Death? Torture? I mean, I figured they might interrogate me... and so, uncertainty returned and fear followed. Terrified once again, I dropped into the bed and cried.

—Thoughts of James Hunter, Hocmar 28, 2134, on the Nirnivian calendar

Chapter 2

Daniel, Ron and several officers sat around the table in the war room. The meeting had barely started. They exchanged greetings, and Nicky read through the agenda for the day. When they at last began the true proceedings, a voice resounded through the interphone. "Commander Ricdeau, sir, Her Holiness is here and she insists on seeing you. She says it's an emergency."

"What the freak?" Ron's lips twisted in a grimace. "The missy stubbed her toe and wants Daddy to kiss the boo-boo? Tell her we're busy—Dan will go talk to her when we're done here."

"Belay that order." A frown formed on Daniel's brow as Tigh fired a dark stare at him. "Rose knows the war room's off-limits even for her. She wouldn't be here if it wasn't important."

"Oh yeah? Shit, how fast do you forget? The little birdie guilt-tripped us into letting her in here like two weeks ago."

Daniel shook his head. "No, that was different. Something bad has happened, I can tell. I feel it my old bones. Listen, Ron, let's see what Rose wants." He smiled. "If I'm wrong, I'll let you win every card game for a year."

After a chuckle, the Koporal smirked. "Fine." He pointed a warning index finger at Daniel's sternum. "But I'll hold you to it. Don't try to weasel out of this one."

Before Daniel answered, the door opened and Rose stepped inside, biting her nails. Though no tears ran down her cheeks, her red eyes guaranteed she'd cried along the way. "Princess, what's wrong?"

"Dad—" Rose sobbed. "It's Hunter."

"Oh... he's not hurt, is he?"

"No, it's worse than that." Another whimper echoed and when she began speaking again, her voice trembled. "Dad, he knows. Hunter knows we lied about the first human. He knows about Miguel. He even knows about the multiverse teleporters."

Stunned, Daniel blinked twice and then his mouth gaped as he froze for a moment.

Ron crossed his arms. "So the boy ain't a complete dumbass after all, huh? If you ask me, we should've capped his ass right from the start."

Rose's sickly complexion grew a shade paler, and Daniel glared at his friend. While he loved that man, the Koporal lacked tact in delicate situations, and that caused problems occasionally. For his response, Tigh shrugged and recoiled. It seemed he decided staying out of the discussion served as the best course of action. A wise choice.

"Ignore him, princess, he's joking. I don't understand— how did James find out?"

Rose gulped. "Miguel contacted him again."

"What?" As he cursed out loud, Daniel clenched his fists. "But we removed his phone—how could the bastard?" A possibility popped into his mind and he snapped his fingers. "The minicomp Janice gave him. No, that doesn't make sense, it can't connect to the GlobalNet."

"Dad, it gets worse." Rose took a deep breath. "When you hung up, I heard Hunter's voice on my phone. Don't ask me how, but he heard part of our conversation."

Adrenaline coursed through Daniel's veins as a cold sweat covered his body. He and Ron shared a glance.

"Nicky, send a tech to investigate Rose's phone ASAP. I don't care how busy they are, tell them to move their asses."

"Yes, sir!" Clicking sounds echoed as Nicky typed on her keyboard. "They're sending someone now. They'll be there in two minutes."

Ron winced. "Dan, if that phone is compromised, that's means—"

"I figured as much." Daniel dismissed the current subject. "Whatever, the techs can handle it. We have to focus on James."

Cheeks reddening, Ron threw his hands in the air. "Why the freak do you worry about the human when the world is going crazy?"

"Because we have to." Daniel swallowed hard. "Don't you see? This is what Doctor Death planned all along. You said it yourself, it's damn suspicious that the multiverse teleporter broke when we sent a team to destroy it. Ron, you were right—the teleporter was already broken. Doctor Death moved it and leaked its location so he'd have proof for James."

"Dear Ulgorack."

"Ron, don't ask me why Doctor Death went to all that trouble, but if he wants James mad at us, I want him to freaking love us. We'll have to explain everything."

"But the Council—"

Before he finished, Nicky interrupted. "Sir! The red phone is ringing."

"Oh crap." The lone line of communication between Daniel and Doctor Death. What a clusterfreak. Prey to a headache, Daniel rubbed his forehead. Whatever Miguel wanted, it concerned what had happened with James. Should he just ignore the asshole? No, he had to address the situation. Under normal circumstances, he took these calls in private, but they were in a hurry, and the phone possessed a useful feature. "Patch it through to the war room, I'll take it here."

Static filled the main screen and then the image displayed Miguel's robotic shape. The cyborg bowed. "Dad, I hope I find you well."

Daniel gritted his teeth. "I told you before, Miguel, you're not my son!"

"Indeed." The president nodded. "Based on Nirnivian tradition, I am not, but I am still married to your daughter."

"Don't remind me."

"My, my, you are so tense. Is it because of my little chat with James?" The emoticon in his eye morphed from a smiling face into a furious glower. "Oh, but my dearest friends, I am afraid that Mr. Hunter's angst is the least of your concerns."

***

On his bed with tears still rolling down his cheeks, James stared at the picture he held in his hand. "Nadia, I... don't get it." With a whimper, he caressed his girlfriend's cheek with his index finger. "I thought she cared about me. Even Miguel said she did, but then how could she? How could she keep me away from you and everyone else, knowing how much I missed you? That goes against everything I thought I knew about Rose, but... she did. She couldn't even try to deny it. She just ran off like a coward. Apparently, I'm not even worth a half-assed explanation to her... Nadia, I... please tell me, what the hell am I supposed to do now? Who can I trust? I can't tell anymore." James sighed. "Well, since I trusted Rose, I guess I never could, huh?" A forced laugh escaped James. "Yeah, that does sound like me."

***

Rose stared at the screen, mesmerized. Time stopped. Seconds became hours; minutes turned into days. Miguel's lone blue eye pierced her soul, familiar, yet so different. Before, it had glimmered with warmth and affection. Now only coldness remained. Overwhelmed by a mix of longing, terror and disgust, Rose felt her head spin, and she wavered on her feet.

"Miguel...," she whispered in a trembling voice.

"Ah, my beloved skeptical angel, it has been months since our last conversation, has it not? I am sorry for being so absent lately." Then Miguel dismissed his own words with a wave. "Oh, but what am I doing apologizing? You are the one who sent me away, are you not, sweetheart?" Rose didn't reply. Instead, she fixated on his image as her breathing sped up. A weakness spread in her legs, and she feared she might collapse at any moment.

***

There was no one in the world Daniel despised more than Miguel. After the pain the disfigured fiend had caused his daughter, how could it be otherwise? Diabo served as a close second, but in comparison, he considered the crimson beast a saint. The instant the cyborg appeared, a yearning for blood awakened deep within. How he wished to grab a toolbox and dismantle the mechanical man, piece by piece, relishing his pleas for mercy the whole time. Alas, the distance between them rendered that dream impossible. Instead of indulging in fantasy, Daniel stepped before Rose, sheltering her from her husband. Then he glared at the screen.

"Stop, leave her out of this!"

"Ah, always your princess's protector, are you not, Daniel?"

"Can't let your ugly mug scare her away."

The emoticon in Miguel's electronic eye frowned. "I have the visage your precious daughter gave me. Dad, if you have a complaint about my face, I suggest you file it with her."

"Cut the crap, won't you!" Tigh pointed an index finger at Miguel. "How the freak did you contact the human? Why? What do you want?"

"So many questions... I shall begin with the first relevant one." Doctor Death shrugged. "I used magic, or rather I might as well have. My methods are far too advanced for your limited intellects. There is no point in explaining the technical details. As for your other two queries, they are linked. In truth, I merely seek to be reunited with my dearest wife. I have missed Rose and desire nothing more than to give her a tender, passionate kiss." The cyborg indulged in a short pause. "Alas, since she took even my mouth away, that wish will forever be unfulfilled and I will have to resort to other displays of affection. What form those will take, I have not decided, but I cannot promise they will be as pleasurable as my initial choice."

The second the vague threat reached Daniel's ears, blood rushed to his face, no doubt reddening his cheeks. He leaned forward, clenching his fists. "I won't let you touch even one hair on her head, you bastard! When Rose told me you were dating, I almost puked. I always knew you were bad news." He gritted his teeth. "I can't believe you won me over for a while. There was a time when I thought you were a devoted husband, but first impressions are right sometimes."

Miguel's smiley displayed a laughing animation. "Ah, Dad, I have missed you. You posed an enjoyable though minor challenge. For the record, I was a devoted husband. When I slipped that ring on her finger, it was as if I ceased to exist. Rose became my motivation and reason to live. Everything I have done, I did for her. Oh, what a vicious reward she gave me."

"I'm tired of the freak's rambling." Ron crossed his arms. "Let's shut him down, he's just messing with us."

"Koporal Tigh, that would be beyond cruel. Will you really hurt the children because you find me annoying?" The president then vanished from the screen as it divided itself into five sections. Each showed an unknown site, all different, yet sharing a common trait: children tied up in chains while swarms of WarBots guarded them. Cold sweat dripped from Daniel's brow. There had been reports of kidnappings in recent months, and the cops remained clueless about the victims' whereabouts and the culprit's identity. He suspected Miguel had revealed the truth behind those crimes.

A second passed, and the cyborg appeared again. "Because of a shipping error, I was overstocked with explosives. Since I ran out of room, I asked my men to store the excess in abandoned buildings. Once they finished that task, I realized with horror that these poor souls somehow ended up restrained in those very locations." He shook his head. "I swear I do not understand how that happened. It is a complete mystery." Miguel grabbed a small device. "By coincidence, I found this not long after. Now, I am not very familiar with these newfangled technologies, but I believe it is a detonator. If you were to upset me, my emotions could grow so intense that my finger would slip and press that delightful red button."

Daniel's eyes grew wide while his mouth gaped. "You're sick! That's a new low. Is there nothing you won't do?"

"Please be careful, Dad, you almost made me slip. Let us return to business. I have a single demand. Though I am certain you can guess, for the sake of completeness, I shall reveal I want Rose. If in two hours you have failed to comply, I will trigger this detonator. You have my word on that." Then Miguel snapped his fingers, resulting in a metallic clink. "Oh, and if I see even one NISDA soldier or any similar professional within twenty miles of those buildings, I promise I will press the button without hesitation. My dearest angel, their young lives are in your hands. Do not let your natural skepticism make you doubt the sincerity of my threat."

Daniel frowned. That Miguel warned them not to mount a rescue operation seemed strange. NISDA couldn't prepare a mission in enemy territory with so little time. Did that imply that the children remained in Nirnivia, against all odds? That made no sense from a tactical perspective. It would seem they faced another puzzle. Daniel swore in silence. How he hated those.

Chapter 3

The sight of Miguel paralyzed Rose. Her limbs and her lips refused to budge, rendering her both immobile and silent. In her mind, visions of flames formed. The same fire that had scorched his body. The same fire in which she deserved to burn. Then the image on the monitor switched from her husband to tied-up kids in various locations. The situation had been horrific before, but now it had reached a whole new level. Rose had to save them somehow. Gritting her teeth, she sidestepped Daniel and faced the cyborg with her hands on her hips.

"Children? Miguel, please, stop this madness. This isn't like you."

"Surrender and I will let them go unharmed."

"Miguel!" Rose's voice, so far weak and trembling, morphed into a shout. "They're kids! You love children and told me you became a surgeon for their sake. Now you will sacrifice them for your selfish designs? Miguel, to see what kind of monster you've become pains me."

The mechanical man shook his head. "I am the monster? Oh, Rose, how delusional of you. How I wish I could ignore reality like you, for it must be quite liberating. If you want to save these children, Rose, then act. Why not solve your own problems for once instead of relying on your father and his army? Surrender and it will be over. Remember, you have two hours starting now." Doctor Death's image vanished as the monitor shut down.

***

The moment the monitor turned black, the special beeper in Daniel's pocket began vibrating. That made him frown. The device allowed Doctor Death and him to share text messages to coordinate calls. Why use it after they'd talked? He grabbed the tool and glanced at the small monochrome screen. Miguel had sent him a GlobalNet address.

"Nicky, can we visit this site safely?"

Daniel handed her the pager, and she nodded. "Yes, sir, our private network is separated from our public GlobalNet connection. That should protect us from any kind of malware the Doctor might've put on there. I'll have it up in a second." After a few keystrokes, the monitor displayed five videos. Each one showed a location where the Ostarkirans held kids hostage. In the top right corner, a counter ticked down, indicating how much time remained.

"Are those live feeds?"

"Looks like it, sir."

Daniel rubbed his chin. "Can you trace the source?"

A nod came from Nicky. "Already on it, sir. It won't take long." A plethora of clicking sounds echoed as she hammered her console.

***

While the technical details eluded Rose, she understood her dad's intent. Cameras filmed those live videos. Trace the source of the stream and you'd find their physical location. Clever, but she doubted that would work. No question, Miguel had envisaged that scenario and set up a countermeasure to stall such an effort. Rose assumed it'd take Nicky hours to get past them. Besides, those kids lay out of reach in Ostark.

Ron apparently shared her skepticism, since he crossed his arms and said, "Dan, they're in another freaking country. Even if we reached them, Miguel would blow them up."

"So what's your plan? Give up?" Daniel groaned. "We have to try."

Rose swallowed hard. The answer presented itself in her mind—it was obvious. Except her father would never agree. Still, she took a deep breath and stepped forward.

"Dad, this isn't right, they're only children. I never thought Miguel would do something this evil. It's unfair. Maybe I should—"

"No! Don't you dare think about surrendering!" Daniel screamed in terror. "I won't lose you. Nirnivia won't lose the Melkar. We'll protect you till the end, no matter what the cost."

"Well, what if we trick Miguel? How about implanting a bug inside me so you can rescue me?"

"No, that's too dangerous. Miguel will expect that. Please understand: you're a priority. NISDA can't risk your life for random hostages."

"But they're children!"

"Yes, and it breaks my heart, but you're too important. Nirnivia needs the Melkar." That twisted logic again. How she hated it. Rose had heard such arguments on multiple occasions, and each time the fallacy grew more senseless.

"Yeah, it's tough, but sometimes we have to make sacrifices," Tigh added in a somber tone. "Oh right, you always had trouble with that part."

"Sacrifices?" Rose yelled while clenching her fists. "You are talking about sacrificing kids! Have you no emotions? And all for these silly wings. Won't it ever end? My husband is my mortal enemy, Brucie's dead, James likely won't ever forgive me and we're about to watch children explode! Damn it, everything is going straight to nothingness!"

"Princess, relax, we'll figure it o—"

"Sir! I've found them. Showing the locations on the screen now." That was faster than Rose had expected. Everyone hushed and focused on this new information. The five addresses weren't just in Nirnivia—they were in the same city as Valardir, though the buildings stood relatively far from each other.

"Wait, what?" Ron scowled. "Why are they so near?" Near wasn't accurate, yet the children were close when considering they should have been in a different country.

Daniel rubbed his chin. "It won't be easy, but if we act fast, we might reach them in t—"

"No, no, no! Dad! If you send soldiers, Miguel will detonate the bombs! He promised, and he won't break a promise made to me. It saddens me, but he meant every word."

"I know, princess, but if we do nothing, they're dead anyway."

Rose grunted in frustration. Her father had a point, but rushing in without thinking would fail. When fighting against Miguel, not using your brain was the worst possible mistake. There had to be another option. Miguel never presented insurmountable scenarios. That wasn't his style. He didn't like brute force. Rather, he stuck a gun to your head, then let you pull the trigger.

Rose had lived with Miguel for years and knew him better than anybody. Puzzles, riddles, mind games—he reveled in those things. Other than science, Kuhard served as his true passion. He could have played for hours without rest, perhaps days. His love for conundrums was incorporated into his strategy. He proved to be a brilliant adversary, though predictable. He would offer a board with an obvious countermove. If you took the bait, he'd crush you not long after. Few experts fell for it, but they couldn't find the correct response either. While victory seemed unattainable, there was always an obscure solution and Miguel even provided subtle hints. If you were smart enough to decipher them, you might turn the odds in your favor and win. No one ever succeeded.

Miguel waged war similarly, and that meant they had a chance. The clear choice was to surrender, but there had to be an alternative. Rose only had to find it. His intelligence trumped hers. Hoping that she could outwit him might be foolish, but she had to try. She replayed the sentences he had uttered, pictured his every movement. A clue lay somewhere. What was it? It eluded her. She had to hurry. After a moment, she burst into laughter. The others looked at her as if she was insane, but Rose didn't care. She'd found the answer.

"I can save them!" Rose exclaimed, overjoyed. "I have to go myself!"

"Rose, you should rest," her father advised with a worried expression. "This is too much for you. You're not thinking straight."

"No, Dad, listen! Miguel said he'd detonate the explosives if soldiers or police officers showed up. I'm neither!"

Daniel sighed and shook his head. "Princess, please stop this madness. You're not making any sense."

"But I am! Miguel chooses his words carefully. He won't do anything if I go."

"Yeah, so?" the Koporal replied before the Commander could. "The rooms are crawling with WarBots. They'd tear you apart. And even if you magically destroy them, you can't reach all five locations in time and we won't risk your life like that. It's a noble thought, Rose, but there's nothing you can do."

"Obviously." Daniel rubbed his chin. "But Rose's logic is sound. I know Miguel too: he won't do anything unless a professional shows up. What if we mount a rescue operation using civilians?"

Ron dismissed the suggestion with a wave. "You're crazy—that ain't gonna work! We can't send amateurs: there are freaking killing machines out there! Anyway, we'd never organize something like that in less than two hours."

"I can do it!" Rose assured with an unsettling smile. "Dad, I can do it! I have a trump card up my sleeve!"

***

A shudder traversed Daniel's body as he repeated Rose's words in his mind. A trump card. Did that imply what he thought? If so, she relied on pure insanity for victory.

"Rose, you can't mean—"

"Don't you understand?" The twisted smile on his daughter's lips widened further. Daniel shivered at the sight. "It's the only way I can reach the buildings in time. Listen, I'm not sure that I can save everyone, but I know I can save most of them. Those machines won't stand a chance. Any surprise Miguel has in store is destined to fail. I'll be safe."

The Koporal fired a questioning stare at Daniel, but he waved his friend away. "Princess, don't do this! Remember what happened before."

"What the freak are you talking about?" Ron shouted with his arms in the air despite Daniel's attempt at shushing him. "Dan, there's nothing she can do!"

"Dad, that was years ago! I was a child myself. Trust me, I can control it."

Could she? In that case, maybe his opposition only doomed the hostages. Daniel grimaced before shaking his head. "Princess, you can't be certain. Sorry, but it's too dangerous." Incapable of looking Rose in the eyes, Daniel averted his gaze. "As Valardir's Commander, I order you be confined to your quarters until this crisis is over. Please forgive me."

***

What a futile threat. Resisting a groan, Rose scanned the area. Several guards watched the scene. Those young, massive and alert men and women answered the call to action by bowing their heads and twiddling their fingers. Though disobeying the NISDA Commander equaled betraying their country, opposing the Melkar equaled heresy, or so many of her followers assumed. Since she remained a mortal woman capable of sin, it wasn't always so clear-cut. Still, going against one's faith demanded courage, and she expected the soldiers delayed as much as possible, hoping a brave soul would escort her out, letting the others off the hook. When she spotted two of them exchanging a glance, she deduced this outcome was about to happen. As anticipated, they stepped toward her, avoiding her eyes and moving so slowly she'd have no problem circling around them unless they picked up the pace.

Rose understood her father's concerns, but she refused to abandon those poor children. She reached for the concealed pocket a talented tailor had added to her dress. In it, her palm seized a soft wood-like object. She knew the material to be synthetic, but it mimicked the real thing well. With a sigh, she pulled out a pistol. Ironically, the one her father had insisted she carry. He might lament that decision now. The two approaching guards wavered, but there was no need to panic. She couldn't harm Daniel or anyone else. Instead, she lifted the gun and soon the cold metal of the barrel brushed against her temple, causing a shiver.

"Try to stop me and lose your"—with a sneer, she performed finger quotes with her lone free hand—"precious Melkar..." The coldness in her voice shocked even her.

The whole room hushed. Everyone stared at Rose, mouths gaping, paralyzed by shock. The silence proved so intense, every little sound reached Rose's ears. The hums of the computers and ventilation system. A small bug that had somehow infiltrated NISDA's most secure complex at its deepest level and now flew around, unaware of the feat it had accomplished. Even the empty paper cup rolling on the floor after Nicky's elbow had bumped into it.

Ron regained his senses first. "She's bluffing!" the Koporal yelled while clenching his fists. "She doesn't have the balls."

Rose squeezed the trigger tighter, more conscious than ever of her rising and falling breasts accompanying every respiration. A tad more pressure and she would cease to exist. "Try me and live to regret it."

***

Daniel's heart beat at a faster pace than ever before. A little more and it might tear through his flesh, escaping his body for Valardir's metallic floor. A voice in his head screamed and yelled about the predicament he faced. His princess...

After a deep inhale, he closed his eyes. Panic led to fatal mistakes. While gritting his teeth, he focused, blocking the madness surrounding him.

Once Daniel regained his calmness, he reopened his eyes and concentrated on Rose. Through his enhanced senses, he spotted so many details. The hunched posture adopted by Rose. Beads of sweat rolling beside her nose. The trembling hand holding the gun. How her pupils dilated. Her scrunched shoulders. Most of all, her breathing. If they tested her, Rose would likely lower her weapon and break down in tears. Ron was correct—she didn't have the balls. And that made sense: Rose feared nothingness, and according to doctrine, suicide guaranteed that fate. Despite his confidence, though, Daniel couldn't act when a chance of being wrong existed. Nirnivia needed the Melkar. He needed his daughter.

"Princess, please, be reasonable."

"Listen!" Desperation tainted Rose's voice. "You know him! To Miguel, this isn't just a war but a mind game, and a game where only one side can win is boring! Often, he put us in seemingly hopeless scenarios that had simple solutions all along. Adding insult to injury, he revealed the answer, but we were blind until it was too late. But this time, I can save everyone."

Daniel shook his head. "Rose, you're wrong. Yes, this is a riddle, but you haven't found the answer. You're playing right into the bastard's hands! Don't you understand? You're doing what he expects you to do. If Miguel were watching, I'm sure he'd be laughing!"

"I don't care!" Rose gritted her teeth as tears flowed down her cheeks. "I won't let children die. I'm so tired of people dying. I can't think of anything else! Yes, it might be a stupid idea, but it's the only one I have and I will try it!"

A curse escaped Daniel's lips. He had seen her like this on rare occasions. Rose performed well under pressure, or at least better than people assumed. However, when pushed too hard, she sometimes snapped. He couldn't reason with her in this state. There was a single person who might persuade Rose, and it was unlikely.

"Rose," Daniel sobbed. "Listen, there's someone I want you to speak with before you do this. I'll go get him. Please don't do anything before I return."

Rose nodded. "Fine, but hurry or I can't guarantee I'll wait."

"Thank you." With that, Daniel stared at Ron while pointing a commanding index finger. "Don't let her out of here." Then he left, running down the corridor.

Chapter 4

I still lay on the bed, but I'd stopped crying. My tears had run out, and the fear became a strange numbness. At that point, I didn't care about anything. So what if I ended up killed, locked up or tortured? I was tired of waiting and wanted them to go ahead with whatever they had planned. As I studied the ceiling filled with emptiness, the door slid open. It didn't matter who it was; I looked out of habit, not interest.

—Thoughts of James Hunter, Hocmar 28, 2134, on the Nirnivian calendar

"James!" Daniel yelled, rushing inside. "Rose is about to do something stupid."

A scoff escaped James's lips. "Yeah, so? That's not my problem."

"My boy, you're confused right now and with good reason." Daniel sighed, then rubbed his brow. "Yes, we lied, but I'll explain everything as soon as possible. Follow me and pretend you've forgiven Rose. Tell her not to go save the children..." James frowned. "Never mind why, I'll explain later."

"Why the hell should I help? For all I know you'll use me, then kill me."

After indulging in a groan, Daniel massaged his temples. "James, think about it: we've sheltered you, fed you. You won't be harmed. Why do you trust Doctor Death so easily? What did that freak do for you?"

"Well, at least Miguel never destroyed a machine capable of sending me home."

I rolled onto my side so I wouldn't see Daniel's face. I wanted nothing to do with Nirnivia. That's when Mr. Ricdeau's wrinkled hands grabbed me and dragged me off the bed. While I considered fighting back, the guard Rose had left behind showed up, and with him there, resistance became hopeless. Daniel warned me to cooperate or he might kill me after all. Part of me yearned to tell him to go ahead, so it'd be over. But I didn't. I guess I wasn't as numb as I thought. Soon, we arrived at the war room, but no sign of Rose except for the shredded remains of a white dress. That upset Daniel, and I had a feeling he'd deduced what had happened. Me, I had no idea. It was strange. I didn't give a rat's ass, and yet I still had a certain morbid curiosity.

—Thoughts of James Hunter, Hocmar 28, 2134, on the Nirnivian calendar

***

When Daniel entered the war room, it took a second or two before he noticed Rose's absence. His heart skipped a beat. Where was she? With a wince, he scanned the area. No sign of his daughter. Plus, none of the officers present acknowledged his arrival. Instead, they remained seated, their mouths gaping. That included Ron. The Koporal preferred to stand when in the war room, but now he slumped in a chair, dazed.

"Ron!" Tigh failed to respond. In fact, he stayed immobile. Not even a single twitch. Daniel almost yelled again, but then he spotted torn white clothes on the floor. Rose's dress. With a gasp, Daniel walked toward his friend, grabbed his shoulders and shook him. "Hey, snap out of it. What's going on? Where is Rose? Why did you let her leave?"

At last, Ron moved, looking up to Daniel. "Dan, it was amazing... she said she was sorry, but she had to go. If she waited anymore, she wouldn't be able to save everyone. We tried to stop her, but"—Tigh frowned—"some kind of light came out of her and she—" His lips twitched as if he disbelieved his own words to come. "She freaking transformed into a goddamn beast. It must be the Papillon. I don't have any other explanation." The various officers nodded in awe. That was when Daniel understood their behavior. Sure, the sudden twist astonished them, yet in their minds, everything was fine now. The Papillon would solve all their problems. Thus they displayed signs of shock yet remained calm.

Unfortunately, Daniel didn't share their enthusiasm. His face reddened with rage as he held his head with both hands. Then he fell to his knees. "Dear Ulgorack! Princess, what have you done?"

"What's wrong, Dan?" Ron hopped to his feet and went to him, resting his palm on Daniel's back. "The Papillon can save those kids—most of them anyway. It's a goddamn miracle!"

A sudden urge to fire off a series of expletives boiled within Daniel, but he somehow resisted. The Koporal wasn't to blame. With Rose adopting that form, nobody could've stopped her. Besides, even if he had been at fault, cursing his name wouldn't help. Swallowing his apprehension, Daniel concentrated on the monitor displaying the five locations. A gigantic creature entered one of them. Rose's rescue attempt had begun.

***

The monster on the monitor hardly reminded me of Rose. It was huge, at least triple her size, and its muscles put Brucie's to shame. Most unsettling, dark blue fur covered its entire body, except for a white spot on the belly. And those yellow eyes freaked me out. Kind of like Diabo's...

The only familiar trait was the long red hair. Ron called it the Papillon. I'd heard that before. Clearing the cobwebs in my mind, I remembered where. A couple months ago, Rose had shown me a painting in the chapel depicting a white-and-cyan creature. Rose explained it was the first Melkar. When in danger, she'd transformed into a powerful being called the Papillon. The book I'd read on Misha had made the same claim. Back then, Rose had assured me she lacked that ability. I guess she had lied, though the animal she had become was nothing like the picture, so maybe not? The Papillon was a majestic crystal being shining with beauty. That beast on the screen was downright hideous and might chomp your head in one bite. It felt wrong for a stunning woman to morph into that atrocity.

—Thoughts of James Hunter, Hocmar 28, 2134, on the Nirnivian calendar

The instant Rose arrived, the machines the others called WarBots attacked. Sprays of bullets flew toward her. To the Papillon, they posed no threat, James soon learned. She dodged with fantastic speed, dancing among the projectiles. His mouth gaping, James's inner voice kept repeating this was impossible.

Once she got close enough to one enemy, the Papillon punched it. Her fist crushed the armor and penetrated the robot's body. Then she jammed her fingers into the hole she'd created and tore the machine in half without breaking a sweat. Nuts and bolts fell to the floor, metallic clinks echoing with each landing. The children gazed upon their rescuer with grateful yet scared expressions. Their cobalt savior terrified them almost as much as their captors, and

James understood why. No doubt he'd share their apprehension were he there.

In the war room, the soldiers cheered, waving and pumping their fists. Morale was up, though James noticed Daniel Ricdeau still refused to celebrate. Instead, the senior observed in silence. Why did the Commander worry so much? Rose dominated and showed no signs of slowing down. In fact, when James's eyes returned to the screen, she had already defeated her foes. He'd missed most of the action. Now, she attacked the chains binding the hostages, ripping them apart while yelling for the children to run to safety.

***

As Rose soared through the air, a powerful wind blew through her newfound fur and it fluttered in the gust. Such an incredible speed she reached. She had flown before but had never come close to moving so fast. Between this pace and the direct route the sky allowed, she might succeed.

A sense of exhilaration merged with Rose's fear and anger. This resulted in a strange mix of emotions, agonizing yet pleasurable. She'd dismantled those machines with her bare hands, ripped the chains apart through her sheer strength. So far, the price had been a mere slight headache. One could get used to this power and relish it, perhaps even become addicted to it like a drug. She dared hope this ordeal would end before that happened to her. At any rate, she needed to focus on her mission. Young lives depended on it.

Soon, Rose spotted the second building below, a dilapidated wooden house built on the outskirts of the city. The overgrown grass, cobwebs and rotting planks suggested it had been abandoned for a while. Gritting her teeth, Rose sped up and plunged toward the nearest window. Two seconds passed, and she crashed through it. Shards of glass cut her flesh as cracking sounds assaulted her ears. A few slivers remained stuck inside her. Warm blood flowed down her brow and her ribs. In retrospect, perhaps she should have smashed through the wall instead. No doubt this form would've been capable of shattering that feeble structure, resulting in fewer bruises. Not that it mattered. The pain proved minimal, a simple warning that failed to convey an emergency. Rather, it indicated a minor issue she shouldn't concern herself with. After all, her wounds had already healed. The Papillon regenerated. When injured, her cells multiplied at a ludicrous rate—what a strange feeling. Nothing could describe it accurately. A tingling sensation, yet so much more.

A WarBot stood beside the window. Without hesitation, Rose punched its singular "red eye" and her whole arm smashed through it. With her fist stuck in the machine, she pulled it out and tore its head in half, freeing herself. One down. The other two detected her presence and opened fire. Streams of bullets moved in slow motion. Rose side-stepped them as she advanced toward the next target. Despite her efforts, a single projectile grazed the side of her chest, lacerating her and staining her cobalt fur crimson. A roar escaped her lips. Not out of pain, but in disappointment over her clumsiness. Still, she reached the second WarBot. A well-placed kick sent it crashing into the wall, broken into pieces. Then a stinging sensation spread through her shoulder. A bullet had hit her. Again she growled, but the resulting hole had closed already. She rushed at the last foe and uppercut him through the roof. Better get the kids out of here before the place crumbled.

***

I'll admit the blue monster scared me. My brain refused to process what I saw and kept telling me I must be having a nightmare. Whatever that creature was, it crushed our War-Bots as if they were toys. After a few minutes, the animal set the children free. Children... that sickened me. I didn't understand why the president had gone that far, and I didn't approve, even if it delivered Rose. I... anyway, eventually, I regained my senses and asked the Good Doctor what was going on. As calm as ever, he answered that Rose had taken charge and transformed into that horror. Back then, I couldn't believe it, and I'm not sure I do now. Historical religious texts claimed that the Melkar became the Papillon. Was that what this beast was? No, that was impossible, and yet I had no other explanation.

—Thoughts of Evelyn Losier, Hocmar 28, 2134, on the Nirnivian calendar

Evelyn applied all the relaxation techniques she had learned. Deep, rhythmic breathing, concentrating on each individual part of her body, recalling pleasant scenes from her past and more. Despite this, her heart rate refused to slow down. In contrast, the mechanical man watched the scene in complete serenity. That annoyed Evelyn. The cyborg should be surprised and distraught. He should be cursing aloud. Rose had ruined his plan. And yet he sat there as if nothing had happened. Then it struck her: he had known Rose possessed such an ability from the beginning. How amazing—he always remained one step ahead of everyone else. His failure to mention Rose's secret irritated Evelyn, but she expected this behavior. He kept his secrets close to his chest.

"So, this was part of your plan?" Evelyn asked, frowning.

The Good Doctor nodded. "We cannot capture Rose while she remains in Valardir, so I lured her out."

"Well, I guess you succeeded, but sacrificing kids?" Evelyn closed her eyes. "That's too extreme for my taste."

"Do not be concerned, for I guarantee no children will die during this operation."

That was a major relief, but I wondered why he was so confident. I mean, a single stray bullet and... still, I trusted the president, even if his claim made little sense. My focus returned to the video feed and Rose. I hated the bitch and wanted her dead. She'd caused this war. If the children hadn't been there, we could have blown her up and watch the Nirnivians mourn their precious Melkar. Except the Good Doctor would have refused. He insisted on capturing Rose, not killing her. Part of me wished to jump him and push the red button. The kids guaranteed I wouldn't, but even without them, his cybernetic body provided amazing speed, and I doubt I would have managed. Ah well, at least I could dream.

—Thoughts of Evelyn Losier, Hocmar 28, 2134, on the Nirnivian calendar

***

Third building, an abandoned warehouse. When Rose slammed through the door, she stumbled and fell to her knees. The ringing in her ears grew unbearable. Without delay, the WarBots inside fired. Since she offered an immobile target, the projectiles found their mark. Bullets tore through her flesh and blood gushed out. Bug bites. Mere bug bites; relax. New puncture wounds opened every fraction of a second, but old ones healed just as fast, undoing the damage.

Somehow, even with the excessive force from the flurry of rounds, Rose managed not to be propelled backward.

With a furious growl, she stood. The kids stared at her with wide eyes. Given that the same gazes had met her in the first two locations, she expected her appearance rather than concern for her safety caused their fear. No matter, focus on the real targets. Rose started running. With every step, she attempted to dodge the enemy fire. Mostly, she failed. More than once, she almost tripped. The roaring in her mind—so distracting. Still, she reached a WarBot. A single punch tore a massive hole in its body and it collapsed. The high-tech electronic now became a pile of junk decorated by electric sparks.

Two left. Rose turned around and... a piercing pain raged through her head. With a whine, she rubbed her temples and kneeled. That thing... that thing in her mind. It surrounded her. Besieged her. As she resisted the enemy within, those outside capitalized on the situation. More and more bullets struck her, transforming her blue body into a muddled mass. Yet she didn't die. Her healing factor struggled, keeping her alive. But the ringing... and the roaring... that presence... that... so hard to focus. Rose needed to get rid of the WarBots. In a moment of pure instinct, she reached for the destroyed robot and ripped off a piece of its armor. She threw it. The improvised disc glided through the air and slid right through a WarBot.

Taking deep breaths, Rose attempted to stand. The flow of bullets from the last enemy sent her back down. She lay on the floor, breasts rising and falling with every respiration. That freaking ringing... that damn roaring... they drove her mad, sapped her energy. A single option presented itself. That ability she sensed within her, but it required tremendous power. It might sap whatever remained of her vitality.

Still, as she glared at the final WarBot, an intense heat filled her eyes. Yellow rays of light emerged from her pupils. Upon contact, the machine melted into an indistinct gray goo. That... hurt a bit. Rose had to rest. Just for a second. Then the kids... yes, the kids... she had to defeat the kids... uh, no, rescue.

***

I watched the battle, drenched in sweat. Those beams... how did she do that? Somehow, Rose transformed into a super strong monster and kicked ass. The whole ordeal reminded me of Japanese anime, or maybe a horror movie with a werewolf or some stupid crap. It was just crazy.
—Thoughts of James Hunter, Hocmar 28, 2134, on the Nirnivian calendar

On the screen, Rose melted the last WarBot and then rested. Less than a minute later, she returned to her feet, alert and moving normally. Without hesitation, she advanced toward the children and severed their chains. That done, she flew through the door.

"Come back, missy." Ron grimaced. "Don't you freaking dare keep going! You can't take it. Three out of five ain't bad!"

Nicky nodded. "She's in terrible shape. If only she had a radio, we could tell her to stop."

"Yeah." Tigh bit his lip, then scowled. "I've been hard on her, always saying she talked a lot but didn't have the balls to act." With a groan, he pointed at the monitor. "Well, I was wrong. She's a goddamn hero."

That was fair, I guess, even if I didn't agree after what had happened. Heh, whatever, I was biased. Anyway, Tigh was right. Rose had barely survived last time. If she didn't stop, she'd... not that I cared at that point. She could rot in hell as far as I was concerned. The others, though, they didn't see it that way. The worst part was, we had no idea if she flew toward the next building or Valardir. No cameras outside, so everyone waited, fidgeting. Before long, Rose popped up on the screen. That answered the question. She tried attacking a WarBot, but they pinned her down.

—Thoughts of James Hunter, Hocmar 28, 2134, on the Nirnivian calendar

"You freaking moron!" Tigh yelled, clenching his fist.

"Don't worry," a trembling voice mumbled. Everyone turned toward the source, the Commander. Daniel offered a sad smile. "She won't die." The old man sounded confident enough despite his weakened appearance. However, based on the tears forming in his eyes, James deduced he didn't consider his prediction a good thing. But why?

***

The ringing... the roaring... that thing closed in on Rose. Resist, must resist. She pushed back, but it shoved her in return. No... no... no... that ringing. That goddamn ringing. It poisoned her mind. No! No! No! Don't! No! Groaaar! Roar! Grrrrrrrrrrr!

***

Still, a flurry of bullets struck Rose, and she regenerated. Daniel swallowed hard. If he was correct, it'd happen soon now. Either that or she'd die. Deep inside, he realized that might be the best alternative, but as Rose's father, he couldn't accept that possibility. She had to live—no, she would live, but at what price? Then the cobalt creature on the screen returned to its feet. Projectiles assailed her, but she paid them no mind. Once standing, she pulled back her head. A guttural roar echoed, far louder than anything she had produced before. The speakers hissed and popped. Daniel and the others covered their ears, wincing. In the building, the windows shattered. The red lens on the War-Bots resembling a single eye cracked. Rose had found her second wind. No, not Rose, but the Papillon. Everyone cheered and pumped their fists. Except Daniel, who instead held his head with both hands. The poor fools... how long had it been since the incident? He lacked the courage to do the simple math, but he remembered Rose had been seven.

Chapter 5

As Daniel carried the basket and the folded blanket, a large smile formed on his face. Before him stretched a blue lake. Well, except for the trees and yellow beams shimmering on its surface. To his right, a wooden pier ventured into the water. Perfect starting point for a bit of canoeing, he supposed, but they lacked a boat and so they'd have to pass. Too bad, the kids might have enjoyed it, and he admitted the exercise would do him good. As Major Kiras had promised, by joining her special team, he had risen through the ranks, but that implied desk jobs filled with paperwork. The newfound sedentary lifestyle put his waistline at risk.

Daniel took a deep breath and fresh air entered his lungs. A pleasant break from the pollution-ridden city. But he'd enjoyed the scenery long enough; they had work to do. He glanced at Madeleine standing next to him. "How about here?"

She nodded. "Yes, it is a perfect spot." With that, Daniel dropped the blanket on the ground, spreading it out while Madeleine planted the parasol she lugged. Laurence had inherited Daniel's pale complexion far more than Janice, so he proved more susceptible to sunburn than both his siblings. Besides this, the kid refused sunscreen. As that thought entered his mind, Daniel turned his head toward the children. The trio chased each other while zigzagging around the trees, giggling. Then birdsong echoed. Rose stopped and looked up. Plenty of multicolored avians filled the air, some flying, some resting on branches. In the distance, Daniel even spotted a cytelicus, one of a species that resembled winged lizards rather than their feathered contemporaries. Soon, the young Melkar's mouth opened as she pointed at a nest. There, a yellow bird fed a worm to its offspring.

Before long, Janice and Laurence joined her and observed the baby, mesmerized. Still, it seemed the scene ended up too boring for Janice's taste, since less than twenty seconds later, she dashed away. Though her chin dipped toward her chest, Rose attempted to follow her sister, but Laurence's leg crossed hers and she stumbled. Lying on her belly, she wailed.

Daniel hopped to his feet and approached them, aiming his index finger at his son. "Laurence!"

The boy presented his palms as a shield. "I am sorry, Dad, I swear I did not mean to."

Daniel grimaced. Based on Laurence's previous behavior, he expected that to be a lie, but the way events had played out, he couldn't be certain that was the case. "That's okay, but be more careful."

"Yes, Dad!"

With that, Daniel crouched beside Rose. The girl rolled onto her side and stared at him with tear-filled eyes. Then she gestured at her elbow. A rock on the ground had caused a small scratch, barely visible. Daniel admitted she was a tad dramatic. Perhaps his pampering encouraged her, as Madeleine suggested, but at Rose's age, he deemed her attitude normal. Yes, Janice and Laurence had both been tougher, but not by much. Besides, Rose was so cute.

"Don't worry, princess, Daddy will take care of it." That said, he picked her up, and she clenched him tight. Without delay, he brought her toward the blanket. Any activity involving children implied a risk of minor injury, so they'd come prepared with supplies. In no time, he cleaned up the wound, kissed it, and applied a bandage. Not that it was necessary, but Daniel realized having one helped calm Rose, and it worked. Her smile returned.

As Daniel dealt with Rose's cut, Madeleine removed the food from the basket. A plate of sandwiches, a bowl of salad, fruits, cookies and more now lay on the blanket. In a rush, Janice and Laurence joined the rest of the family to eat. Without delay, Rose grabbed a cookie while licking her lips. Daniel knew she'd "helped" Madeleine bake them. Well, if you considered covering the kitchen in a flour-related mess helping. He figured tasting a pastry she'd contributed to provided some level of excitement. Before Rose sampled the treat, Laurence shoved her. He put little strength into the push, as he wasn't foolish enough to hurt her in front of his parents. Still, Daniel refused to ignore the hostility behind the gesture.

"Hey!" the boy shrieked. "What are you doing? Those are mine!" With a whimper, Rose offered Laurence her precious snack, but he slapped her hand away. "You want to infect me with your germs?"

Daniel glared at his son. "Laurence!" That deserved a scolding, and he would provide one. Or so he planned, but then Madeleine squeezed his shoulder.

"Oh, it is only children acting as children do, dear. My darlings, there is no need for bickering. We brought plenty of cookies for everyone, so, Laurence, stop pestering your sister." A scowl wrinkled her brow. "However, Rose, you are aware of the rules. You must eat a proper meal before dessert."

Daniel dismissed the notion with a wave. "Ah, come on, it's a special occasion. Let her have it backward just this once."

"I suppose that is fine." Madeleine waggled a lecturing index finger. "But do not make a habit of it, young lady."

After a pleased grin, Rose sank her teeth into her cookie. "Yummy!"

"Now, Rose, what did I tell you about eating with your mouth closed?"

"Sorry, Mommy!"

While well intentioned, the apology resulted in her breaking the rule again. That brought a chuckle out of Daniel as he reached for a sandwich. A deafening roar made him pause midway, and a shiver ran down his spine. Poor Rose dropped her precious cookie. Worried, Madeleine bobbed her head toward the source and said, "Daniel!"

Without a sound, he rested his index finger against his lips. She stilled her tongue. There wasn't any need to draw his attention—he'd already noticed. Several feet away, near a rare blue priss, a large brown beast glared at them. Its roar revealed razor-sharp fangs while drool dropped on the soil. Those complemented the terrifying claws on its paws. A morglar, no doubt about it. The size alone clued Daniel in to that fact, and if it had not, the missing patches of fur in its otherwise luxurious coat would have. The radiation caused by the old war had hit morglars hard and introduced that mutation to their species. While they avoided Gorumars, they possessed immense strength and could kill a person with ease if provoked, or hungry enough. Based on the copious amount of salivating, Daniel assumed this one starved, a bad sign.

Janice glanced at Daniel. "Daddy!"

"It's okay, sweetie, he won't hurt us." Though he lied, he prayed the children believed him. "Pretend you're dead and he'll go away."

Daniel had no idea if that was accurate. Tons of sources ranging from the GlobalNet to TV shows swore by it. Apparently, the animals refused to eat anything they didn't slay themselves. Still, it sounded like an urban legend, a feeling that increased tenfold when such a beast entered your sight.

As he gestured for his family to lie down, Daniel reached for his concealed pistol out of instinct. His hand grabbed air instead of the desired weapon. Why bring a gun to a pleasant picnic? Would the bullets meant for a Gorumar have worked on a morglar? A futile question, but he wondered anyway.

Since Daniel was unarmed, he figured he should join the others. That was when he realized Rose had left the blanket. The child stepped toward the morglar. He almost screamed her name, but a bright light emanating from her body interrupted him. Daniel spun his head and shielded his eyes with his palm. Rose's limbs grew bigger and her dress began to rip. Soon, the expansion tore the fabric to shreds. A shudder ran down Daniel's spine. Between that and his churning stomach, he had a bad feeling.

Once the brightness vanished, Rose wasn't Rose anymore. A strange hideous creature had replaced her. Blue fur coated the monstrosity except for a white patch on her belly. Despite her small stature, she bulged with muscles. As for her feathery wings, they'd morphed into distorted black appendages that would forever haunt Daniel's nightmares. Her irises became yellow, her teeth sharp as knives.

With a gaping mouth, Madeleine stared at their daughter before uttering a single word: "Papillon!"

Like every Nirnivian, Daniel had heard of that legend. When in danger, the original Melkar had transformed into a divine creature named Papillon. Daniel had seen paintings and drawings, but the thing in front of him looked different. The Papillon appeared graceful and crystal-like; this beast was clumsy in comparison and covered in fur. Daniel understood that after thousands of years, artists couldn't deliver an accurate depiction. Still, the cobalt brute didn't seem holy... and yet, didn't Ulgorack teach that appearances were deceitful?

The Papillon glared at the morglar. As if to warn the animal, she let out a nerve-wracking scream and Daniel covered his ears. The morglar released a chilling howl of its own, but it lacked impact in comparison. Perhaps doubting its chances, the famished fiend wavered and stepped away. Too late. The hallowed being rushed toward the intruder. Once close, she struck the morglar with an uppercut right to the chin. The blow propelled the poor creature three feet back. Blood joined the saliva dripping from its jaws. Undeterred, it returned to its paws and jumped forward, swinging his claws at the Papillon. Before the sharp nails scratched her, however, she aimed another punch. Again, the morglar collapsed. This time it didn't get back up.

With another roar, the Papillon dashed for the carcass and pummeled it with both punches and kicks. Each blow drew more blood as gashes and sores covered the corpse. Pale as snow, Madeleine observed the scene, unable to avert her gaze, much like Daniel. Janice clutched her mom's leg as if for dear life and cried. "Stop! Rose, it's already dead!" she yelled. As for Laurence, he remained quiet, though he held his mother's hand for comfort.

Despite Janice's pleas, the Papillon kept striking the morglar's cadaver. With a hard swallow, Daniel stepped toward it and said, "It's okay, princess, it can't harm us anymore."

The Papillon growled and glared at him. Ah crap. Daniel attempted to retreat, but the cobalt creature hopped forward and punched him in the gut. A squeal escaped Daniel's lips as a single tear rolled down his face. Then he fell to his knees. That was by far the strongest hit he'd ever endured. The monster then jabbed him in the nose. It broke, blood dripping down his mouth and cheeks. Daniel dropped to the ground. Paralyzed by pain, he couldn't move, let alone stand up. The Papillon moved so fast even his miraculous vision failed to track her.

Janice shouted, "No! Don't hurt Daddy!"

Alerted by the sound, the Papillon focused on the spectators. Though they were her family, such relations lacked meaning for the holy being. She snarled at them. Driven by fear, Daniel somehow stood up. Again, he attempted to seize his hidden gun, only to realize its absence. What did it matter? He couldn't have pulled the trigger. That brute was his daughter. Perhaps not on a biological level, but she was his daughter, not to mention the Melkar. What was he supposed to do? Murder her? If he couldn't, would his wife and other children die?

As he fought the conflicting emotions, Daniel seized a rock. Maybe he could knock her out? Gritting his teeth, he lifted his improvised bludgeon. The Papillon sensed his movement and landed a hook, shattering his jaw. Then a vicious kick sent him flying. This time, he knew he was down for the count. Rose glowered at the others and took a couple hesitant steps. Daniel struggled to get up, but to no avail. The attacks had ravaged his body, so he went for the last remaining option: prayer. Papillon roared, ready to pounce... then she wailed, holding her head with both hands. The beast began to collapse. A naked Rose dropped in the grass.

Pallid and weeping, Laurence yelled, "I told you she was bad! I told you!"

That day had been a tragedy, but it had ended better than Daniel had hoped. Madeleine had called for help and he had been taken to a hospital. Though severe, the injuries had healed quicker than expected. Unfortunately, Rose remembered the whole ordeal. She kept apologizing in tears and swore she'd wanted to stop but couldn't. Daniel and Madeleine understood it wasn't her fault, but she'd blamed herself. They'd reassured her as best they could, and she'd more or less recovered.

The children, God bless them, weren't so forgiving. Janice grew terrified of her little sister and didn't dare approach her. The beautiful friendship they'd shared since the basement episode had disappeared. Thank Ulgorack, after a few months, Janice had come to understand that Rose had tried to protect them and they'd become closer than ever. As for Laurence, he'd despised Rose from the start, and that hadn't changed.

Daniel and Madeleine pondered whether they should disclose the incident. Rose's metamorphosis could serve as definitive proof that she was the holy prophet, but the public might condemn the senseless violence she'd committed. As a kid, maybe Rose couldn't command the Papillon yet. However, records showed her predecessor had transformed when she was four, three years younger than Rose, and she had maintained perfect control.

After weeks of indecision, they'd resolved to hold their tongues. To hide the truth, they'd blamed Daniel's condition on a morglar attack and covered up the catastrophe. Silencing the children had posed a challenge, but they'd managed. Even today, Laurence kept the secret, though Daniel failed to understand why. They'd explained to Rose that she shouldn't use the Papillon again, but she hadn't needed convincing. She had sworn she never would, no matter what. And she hadn't—until now.

Chapter 6

Rose pulled one hell of a comeback. After being pinned down for several minutes, she shrugged it off and got up. And she meant business. That roar broke the windows, for crying out loud.

—Thoughts of James Hunter, Hocmar 28, 2134, on the Nirnivian calendar

Though bullets kept striking the Papillon, she showed no signs of urgency. Instead, she walked toward the closest WarBot at a deliberate yet determined pace, staring it down. Every step possessed such strength, James could have sworn the ground shook with each one. In response, the WarBot continued assailing her with streams of projectiles, to no avail. The effort failed even to slow the cobalt beast. Once within reach, she grabbed the WarBot's left machine gun and ripped it out of its socket. Then she impaled the cracked red "eye" with it, putting such force into the blow that the weapon traversed the robot's whole body and, among a multitude of sparks, it collapsed.

Without delay, Rose tore off the second machine gun. With another growl, she turned toward her next target and threw it. The improvised javelin soared through the air. Her aim perfect, it pierced through this WarBot as well. Two out of commission; a lone adversary remained. Rose had no intention of messing around. She lifted the body of the fallen foe lying beside her and flung it at the last enemy. Upon contact, a metallic cacophony echoed. James covered his ears and winced. Once the sound relented, he realized the battle was over.

That was quick! I admit, it was impressive, and scary too. Anyway, Rose had to hurry. The countdown had almost reached zero. With a heavy heart, I understood she'd lost any chance of rescuing the children in the fifth building. How tragic... still, it could've been far worse. Or so I thought. Instead of freeing the kids, Rose glared at them. What was going on? Then she approached them, roaring. That was when Nicky said the red phone was ringing again.

—Thoughts of James Hunter, Hocmar 28, 2134, on the Nirnivian calendar

***

Beads of sweat rolled down Daniel's brow as the Papillon dispatched her foes. That efficiency. That ruthlessness. No, that wasn't Rose. Shivers assailed him. His old aggressor had returned. And in the presence of kidnapped children. Then the beeper in his pocket, the one allowing the exchange of text messages with Doctor Death, vibrated. What perfect timing. After mumbling a curse, he fished it out and read the following words: "Answer right away or she's dead." On cue, Nicky said, "Sir, we're getting another call from the red phone."

Daniel grimaced. While he doubted even Miguel's bombs could vanquish the Papillon, he figured he should be prudent. "Transfer it to the main screen."

"Sir?"

"Do it."

As instructed, Nicky pressed a few buttons on her keyboard. Static covered the monitor, obscuring the view of the cobalt monster approaching the children. Then Miguel's metal body replaced the nightmarish scene. The cyborg offered a slight bow. "Thank you for kindly taking my call despite the crisis you are facing, Dad. Sorry, I always forget you dislike that mark of affection. Regardless, the two hours are almost up, yet I have not heard from my lovely wife. I assume that implies she rejected my offer." He shook his head. "Ah well, that is her choice. Alas, I am a man of my word and so will fulfill it when the last few remaining seconds have passed. Oh, but what am I talking about? The timer ran out while I spoke." With that, he pushed the detonator's button. Daniel braced himself while he shuddered. Darkness filled the screen as the lights surrounding Doctor Death shut down. Then the room lit up again.

Ron Tigh frowned. "What the freak?"

"I have warned you that we installed explosives in those buildings, and that is true—I am not a liar. Check for yourself if you desire. I have also threatened that I would activate this detonator after two hours if Rose refused to surrender, and I did. However, I never pretended the detonator is for the bombs in the buildings. Those explosives are disarmed and harmless." The cyborg pointed at the detonator. "As for this instrument, well, I converted it into a light switch."

The realization struck Daniel like a blow. With a gasp, he recoiled, rubbing his brow. Miguel had fought a bitter war against them. He'd committed many atrocities over the years, but he still had a code of honor. Despite this, they'd expected the worst from him, and now they'd paid the price. The kids had been in no danger, at least not until Rose used her power. While she'd correctly deduced Miguel played one of his mind games, she'd failed to grasp its nature. They all had. As Daniel had predicted earlier, she'd walked straight into their nemesis's trap.

"Since you are worried about the children's fate, how about we check on them?"

Miguel reached for something. As he pulled the object forward, Daniel recognized the shape of a minicomp. The president shoved the small screen before the videophone's camera. The Papillon pummeled a dead child. Tears overcame Daniel as he averted his gaze. How could Rose? Then Tigh's voice echoed. "What kind of clusterfreak is this? They're goddamn robots!"

For a moment, Daniel ignored those words, choosing to keep wallowing in despair. When the implication struck him, his heart skipped a beat. His eyes widened. Holding his breath, he lifted his neck and stared at the monitor. No blood covered the slaughtered kids. Instead, severed wires and gears served as their guts. Machines wrapped in a fake skin more realistic than he'd have imagined possible.

Miguel pulled the minicomp out of view and shook his head. "Dad, you and my dearest angel know I love children. I have dedicated my life to saving theirs, and yet you were so eager to believe that I would murder all those kids for my own devices. This begs the question: am I the monster you assume, or are you projecting your own darkness onto me? This could be an interesting debate, but you have your hands full with other matters... perhaps at a later date."

"Wait!" Daniel presented his palm. "What about those kidnappings we've been hearing about?"

The Doctor shrugged. "How should I know? Am I supposed to be in charge of the Nirnivian police? Frankly, if you are interested, discuss the matter with them. I am far too busy to solve an unrelated mystery. Besides, I suggest for the moment that you focus on the crisis at hand." He waved. "Ta-ta!"

The screen went blank. As his heart rate increased, Daniel wavered. He stumbled toward a chair, almost collapsing. There he sat, on the brink of hyperventilation. A splitting headache assailed him. Though he attempted to massage his temples, that provided no relief. Fingers touched his shoulder. He turned his head. They were Ron's.

"Dan, I'm so sorry." Unable to muster the courage to speak, Daniel nodded. "You knew this would happen, didn't you?"

Daniel closed his eyes and indulged in deep respiration. "Yes, you could say that. Rose transformed when she was seven and she attacked me." The Koporal's lips moved as if about to ask a question. Daniel kept going. "Never mind, it's a long story and there's no time." Adrenaline rushing through his veins, Daniel hopped to his feet and glanced at a young officer manning a console. "Nathaniel!" The soldier straightened and saluted. "Can you still track Her Holiness?"

"Let me check." A few keystrokes followed. "Yes, sir!"

That was good. After Rose had escaped to rescue James when he'd arrived, NISDA had implanted a tracking bug in her body without her knowledge or consent. That deception had happened during one of her physicals. They hadn't asked her permission because they'd figured she'd refuse. No doubt a dubious move on their part in terms of morality, but now it served as their lone advantage.

Ron grimaced. "Dan, sorry to bring this up, but I'd guess I was right about the traitor."

"Yes, there's a good chance we have a spy among us. If so, we'll find him soon. But if anyone can pull something like this off without a mole, it's Miguel. Making us believe there's a traitor by managing the impossible is in his style. Then we'd suspect everyone and..." Daniel dismissed his own comment with a wave. "Whatever. Ron, I'm leaving you in charge of Valardir. Have the techs inspect James's minicomp in addition to Rose's phone. Might as well have them do a whole system check just in case Doctor Death snuck viruses into our mainframe."

"Sure, Dan, no problem, but"—the Koporal frowned—"where are you going?"

It all seemed so surreal. Daniel winced. "I never thought I'd say this, but I'll assemble a squad and we'll hunt down the Papillon. Rose is my daughter, so she's my responsibility."

***

Diabo called for me. Didn't tell why; sounded urgent. Hurried.

—Thoughts of Wrathchild, Hocmar 28, 2134, on the Nirnivian calendar

When Wrathchild arrived, Diabo gawked at a small TV. Static obscured the image and white noise distorted the sound. Whatever program he watched held his complete attention. He stared at the screen, unwavering. The red beast didn't even look at her, though he waved.

"Wrathchild! 'Bout time." The boss pointed at the monitor. "Check this shit out." She did. A scowl formed on her brow as her mouth gaped. A blue animal stomped down a city street, roaring. People ran away in panic as they shrieked. Despite this, some failed to escape. The creature seized them and tossed them aside like dolls. Or it punched them to death. What a bloody massacre. The grotesque sight would have turned Wrathchild's stomach if she hadn't been so used to carnage. She blinked, and when she reopened her eyes, the cobalt brute jammed her fist into a car's roof. The metal bent under the pressure, windows shattering into shards. Wrathchild figured it was a monster movie, but she didn't understand why Diabo was showing it to her.

At that moment, a journalist said, "This is Natalie Welling for MegaNews. Based on anonymous sources, the creature destroying our city is in fact Her Holiness, who transformed into the Papillon. This sounds ridiculous, but we received a video showing the creature coming out of Valardir. Also, the red hair matches Her Holiness's. If it's true, we have no idea why she's doing this, but we will keep you informed as we learn more. Residents of the Talar block should evacuate. Avoid the creature at all costs. If you s—" She frowned. "My minicomp has just received a message." A gulp came from the reporter. "Valardir officials just confirmed the reports are true. What this—" A gasp echoed. "Oh dear God, no!" With a growl, the assumed Papillon rushed forward, growing in size as it approached. It lifted its arm and sliced with its claws. The image turned sideways. Melissa figured the camera had fallen. Then the annoying static filled the screen completely.

Rose? No, couldn't believe. Rather, didn't want to. Heart sank. Wasn't like her. Besides, didn't know could transform. Why attack own people? Rose nice woman, not murderer. Sorry for reporter. Young; just some kid. Poor girl took risk hoping big break.

—Thoughts of Wrathchild, Hocmar 28, 2134, on the Nirnivian calendar

"Rose?" Wrathchild brought her hand to her forehead. "Can't be!"

A nod came from Diabo. "Yeah, never thought I'd see her on a rampage; ain't making no sense. Damn, she's strong... and freaking fast. Maybe faster than you. Shit, I figured we hit the jackpot with Allison, but that thing got her beat." He rubbed his chin. "That bastard's like the ultimate living weapon..."

Made me shiver. Tried reassure self. No way he'd... too crazy, even for him.

—Thoughts of Wrathchild, Hocmar 28, 2134, on the Nirnivian calendar

Chapter 7

I was so confused. The bombs weren't armed; the kids were never in danger. It didn't make sense.

—Thoughts of Evelyn Losier, Hocmar 28, 2134, on the Nirnivian calendar

A severe headache split Evelyn's brain as she replayed the conversation between the president and Daniel Ricdeau. While she rubbed her brow, she glanced at the Doctor. "What's going on?" Though it was not her intention, a touch of frustration lingered in her voice.

"That is simple, Evelyn. I would not intentionally harm a child." The cyborg bowed his head. "While I admit children have sometimes died during raids, those were accidents. There was no point in endangering the kids to ensure success—we only needed to convince our enemies the threat was real."

Evelyn rubbed her chin. "Fair enough, I didn't want them hurt either. But you don't seem surprised by Rose's transformation. You knew what would happen, didn't you?"

"Rather, I knew it was likely. It would have been preferable for Rose to surrender, but I never expected she would make it that easy for us. Daniel Ricdeau would not have allowed it. As for Rose's metamorphosis, she revealed that fascinating ability during our marriage. While this is not the best outcome, it is a major victory."

"I don't see how."

The president shrugged. "That is because you keep your eyes closed! Our target is now outside the military complex that prevented us from reaching her. While I concede that capturing Rose in this form might be impossible, we can make an attempt. Even in the case of failure, consider this: Rose is killing Nirnivians. The government cannot conceal her actions. No need to foresee the future to realize unpleasant consequences will follow. Whatever they might be, Rose will have to live with them, and I suspect they will render Nirnivia unstable." Miguel formed a fist. "What weakens our enemy strengthen us."

"All right, but how did you know Rose would—" A grimace twisted Evelyn's lips. "I mean, it's not like her to be so rash."

"Mere psychology, dear Evelyn, mere psychology," the cyborg explained while waggling a lecturing finger. "Predicting people's reactions is not that difficult if you observe them well. We are who we are and behave as such."

Evelyn shook her head. "That's bullshit! There are countless examples where someone has acted uncharacteristically."

"Perhaps on the surface. Occasions where a person behaved in an unusual manner exist, but they are far rarer than believed. If someone appears to act uncharacteristically, it is because your assumptions concerning that person's mind are incorrect. Grasp the psychology behind the Gorumar, and predicting their actions becomes easy." The Doctor dismissed his own comment with a wave. "No, I oversimplify. Rather, a collection of probable actions can be deduced. Then it is a matter of assigning a probability to each possibility and adjusting your plan in accordance. Pardon the gloat, but I excel at that game."

That was true. Almost nothing caught him off guard. He was on top of everything. And he used his psychological tricks on me. More often than not, it worked, though he needed to be familiar with the "victim." While I didn't doubt the president's skills, his plan relied too much on blind luck for my taste. Sure, it had succeeded, but by chance, and I told him so.

—Thoughts of Evelyn Losier, Hocmar 28, 2134, on the Nirnivian calendar

The smiley in the cyborg's electronic eye engaged in a laughing animation. "Oh, but I assure you I was certain of the results. I gamble, but only when the risk is minimal." He paused. "Tell me, when you gaze in the mirror, are you ever surprised by your reflection's movements?"

"Of course not! It does whatever I do."

"In other words, you can guess your reflection's every move without a mistake?"

"That's a strange way of putting it, but yes." A giggle escaped Evelyn. "Anybody can, it's nothing special!"

"Rose is my reflection, figuratively speaking. Remember, I am her husband and I lived with her for years. I know her better than anyone, including herself, so I can predict her actions with uncanny accuracy." He brought his hand to his speaker. "Rose is a smart woman, but she has peculiar quirks. In particular, the isolation she suffered because of her special status had a clear effect. Part of her personality never fully matured. The result is she occasionally behaves like a child in an adult's body. Despite this, she can use her head just fine, and while she's not a genius, her intelligence is above average.

"But that is unimportant—the crucial matter is that Rose has a major weakness. She is governed by emotions. I have told her so, but she did not listen. When Rose is pushed, she decides with her heart without regard for reason. Passionate behavior often leads to atrocious consequences.

For Rose, those kids dying was insufferable. Under normal circumstances, she would not use the Papillon, for she fears it. At a young age, she almost murdered her adoptive father while transformed. However, I realized that if I pushed her enough, she would attempt such a foolish rescue. This is where James comes in." His emoticon then switched to a nervous expression.

"I feel bad for using him, and I hope he does not come to harm because of me. Rose is fond of James. She calls him her best friend, but it goes beyond that, and I do not mean romance. She cares for the man more than she should considering she barely knows him. I believe it is in part because, as a human, he reminds her of a happier time. I orchestrated a fight with James so that Rose would be in a 'favorable' state of mind. While I doubt Diabo intended to help me, Brucie's death also proved invaluable. The poor bodyguard's demise allowed me to proceed earlier than expected. For once, I must thank Mr. Pierre Garland.

"Those events traumatized Rose. From her perspective, her life is shattering. It is an overreaction, but she cannot stop herself, for she is how she is, like everyone else. I foresaw that, given her situation, she would wish to save those kids even more. Everything is wrong and out of her control, but for once Rose could do something. For once, she could prevent the tragedy. Armed with this knowledge, I compiled a list of ten courses of action she might take. Three were probable. The first two options were that she would transform or surrender to me. I estimated those alone accounted for ninety-four percent of probability. That she would use the Papillon was far more likely, so I did not expect her to surrender—not yet. The third alternative was that she insisted her father send soldiers despite my threats, which, combined with the first two options, brought the odds up to ninety-nine point eight percent. This would have been the worst choice for us, but I prepared a contingency plan. The other seven possibilities were so far-fetched that I judged them insignificant. At any rate, in fact, we might capture my dearest angel by the end of the day. I have men deployed in Nirnivia for this purpose. While my plan achieved total success, I cannot take full credit, for I owe a debt to my friend James. The poor fool is my deus ex machina. He appeared in this world out of nowhere just to help me, though he did not intend to."

That made more sense than I had given him credit for, but I still wasn't convinced. It was too uncertain—too random. At least then I understood why he bothered with the human punk.

—Thoughts of Evelyn Losier, Hocmar 28, 2134, on the Nirnivian calendar

Evelyn bit her lip as her frown intensified. "Sorry, Good Doctor, but it's still too much of a gamble for me."

"Only because you do not accept the reality of psychology. I admit that it is an unpleasant concept. We like to believe we are more than we are. That is the reason why every society has invented a god. We were created by a mastermind and have a purpose. Ergo, we are important. Those are comforting thoughts, but a mere delusion. We are insignificant beings in an enormous multiverse we do not understand. In the grand scheme of things, our lives are nothing but a joke. That is not heartening, so I do not blame you or anyone else for refusing to acknowledge these facts." The mechanical man averted his gaze and fell silent for a second. "There was a time when I did the same..."

"No, it's not just that." Evelyn gritted her teeth. "There are holes in your plan that don't involve psychology."

"Such as?"

"Well, you had James overhear a conversation where Rose said NISDA destroyed a multiverse teleporter. Great, but how could you tell Daniel Ricdeau would call her? How could you achieve perfect timing? He could've been too slow. How did you know Rose would reveal their intentions? Or that she'd go to the war room after the fight with James? Seems like blind luck, and you're too careful to depend on that."

The president nodded. "You are correct—I was lucky. However, I did not rely on fortune alone. Evelyn, remember that Rose is my reflection. To determine that she'd request her father contact her once the mission was completed demanded little effort. I monitored her phone and so could tell when their conversation started. As for how I deduced Rose would head for the war room—well, what else would she do? Daniel spoiled and sheltered her all her life. It is only natural that she sought his aid when faced with a crisis."

Evelyn rubbed her chin. "No, I don't buy it. It's still too random. There's no way to know what will happen now. Rose could transform back any minute. And if she doesn't, what's stopping her from tearing through our troops?"

"While I cannot offer any guarantee, it is doubtful Rose will be able to transform back. Based on the story she told me, I deduce that as a child she only transformed back due to exhaustion and not a desire to protect her father. If I am correct, then she will remain the Papillon until her energy is drained. Of course, I could be wrong, but I am of the opinion this will take far longer now that she is an adult. As for her tearing through our troops, she most definitely can, but I assure you I took this into consideration and came prepared."

Evelyn grimaced. "Capturing her is still a long shot with the Nirnivian soldiers running around."

"Indeed, but at least we have a chance. If we fail, which is more probable than I'd like to admit, Nirnivia will be in turmoil, making future capture attempts easier."

A frown wrinkled Evelyn's brow. "And what if Rose had rescued the children before she lost control?"

"Ah, but that would have been the most favorable scenario. No question, Rose would then have transformed back without delay, out of fear of losing control. Since I forbade for NISDA troops from being within twenty miles of each building, picking her up before they showed would have been simple."

Evelyn scoffed. "To think, after all that talk about how Nirnivia isn't the enemy, you basically declared war against them, whether we capture Rose or not."

"Not if they wish to live, a truth they are aware of. And if their foolishness trumps their survival instinct, then I am grateful for their stupidity." The emoticon in Miguel's eye adopted a furious frown. "My ethics prevent me from exterminating Nirnivia unless strictly necessary, but if they insist on restarting the hostilities after I have been more than generous about their own transgressions, I deem our response self-defense. We shall crush them and take my beloved by force."

"But... no, this is too insane, even for you. There are so many ways it can backfire." Then Evelyn's eyes widened, and she gasped. "Unless... dear God, you know what will happen! I can't explain how, but you do! That's why you went ahead with this insane plan."

"Are you suggesting I am a prophet capable of foreseeing the future?" Again, his emoji burst into laughter. "Ah, Evelyn, let me assure you, I leave those kinds of things to my wife." Miguel shrugged. "Alas, I am a mere mortal incapable of performing divine feats. Now, I am confident there are other weaknesses you could highlight in my scheme, but I am bored with this. It worked out and that should satisfy you."

The Good Doctor had a point. I didn't approve of his methods, but the president got results again and again; that was the important part. He won a major victory that day. If we succeeded, the war was over. Yet he didn't seem happy.
    —Thoughts of Evelyn Losier, Hocmar 28, 2134, on the Nirnivian calendar

"Good Doctor, I'm sorry if I'm out of line, but considering what you've accomplished..."

"Do you deem my enthusiasm underwhelming? If so, you are correct." The cyborg closed his remaining biological eye. "I was married to Rose for years before she tried to murder me and cursed me with this broken body. Despite this, I still have feelings for her. Rose is a woman like no other, Evelyn. What happened today will bring her great pain, and that saddens me." The mechanical man crossed his arms. "This is not the worst of it. Rose knows me as I know her, and she believed I would kill those children. Though I should not care about the opinion of a mad person, it hurts me." Miguel paused for a moment. "Regardless, by nightfall, Rose might be our prisoner, and that is cause for celebration. At least her fragile mind will receive another shove. No matter what comes next, the future should be interesting."

***

I need your help. Simply put, The Cyborg's Crusade ran out of budget. Now, books 5 and 6 will be released, but after that, I simply don't have the money to continue. The good news is that book 6 is the end of the first arc of the series, so a lot of plot threads will be resolved. However, there are still many that won't be. I want to continue, I really do, but editing costs are very high, which is fair given the hard work needed.

So, if you enjoy this series and would like to see it run to its conclusion, I need your help. How can you help? Well, buy the books. If you already did, you've already done more than I expected anyone to and I thank you.

Also, I'm planning to do a crowdfunding campaign later. It probably won't be for a while, so please join the fan club so you can be informed when it happens.
https://thecyborgscrusade.com/fanclub.html

How can I help even more?
- Leave a review on Goodreads and retailers like Amazon, Kobo, Barnes and Noble, Apple books and Google books
- I don't expect anyone do to more than buy books, but if you want to:
- You can recommend the series to friends/family/acquaintances who enjoy sci-fi/fantasy
- You can buy books as gifts for friends/family/acquaintance
- If you've already bought the book and want to contribute even more, feel free to buy some merch. I don't expect anyone to do this, but if you prove me wrong, I won't complain. Visit the fourth wall store here: https://merch.thecyborgscrusade.com/

- With merch, a large part of the money goes to the merch production cost. If you'd like your contribution to go fully to The Cyborg's Crusade books, I'm working on a subscription service where you can get early access to content and bonuses. https://thecyborgscrusade.com/premiumfanclub.html

- Finally, I hate doing this, but the merch store allows it, so if you don't want merch, or a subscription, you can donat. I don't like receiving something for nothing, but this way your contribution does go fully to The Cyborg's Crusade books. https://merch.thecyborgscrusade.com/en-cad/pages/donate

Since the end might be near, I want to take a moment to show you some gratitude. Thank you so much for reading my books. Truth is, this is a passion project I never intended to publish. I'm just an anxiety-ridden guy who never dared really to put himself out there. That's why I decided to publish, because it's something really hard to do for me and I realized I needed to push myself forward. So, really, this was a self-improvement project. I never expected to sell one copy. I sold over a hundred. Eight people enjoyed it enough to preorder the fifth book. While that's not nearly enough to cover future editing costs, it's more than I ever dared imagine. Thank you so much.

As far as I'm concerned, even if it ends here, The Cyborg's Crusade has been a success. I put myself out there, and it didn't kill me. Good enough. I even made some really bad videos I uploaded to YouTube and other social media! For me, that's incredible. Just five years ago, it would have been unbelievable. So, I'm satisfied. But, there are a few people out there who seem to enjoy this series.

And yeah, they are very few. But, they are still there and I know how it feels to have a story you enjoy never reach its conclusion. And so, I have to try everything I can to finish it.

ABOUT THE AUTHOR

My name is Benoit Lanteigne and I'm a French Canadian (outside of Quebec) who's trying to write in English. That can be tricky. I'm a computer programmer and I enjoy it. I see many inspiring writers who hate their day jobs and hope to quit someday, but that's not my case. Mostly, I've worked on websites and web applications.

Back in school, I enjoyed writing and according to my teachers and classmates; I had a talent for it. Well, not so much for grammar and spelling, but they liked my stories. Once I went to university, I dropped writing as a hobby. There were other things I wanted to focus on, such as my career. Then, in the early 2000s, around 2006 I'd say, I had a flash of inspiration. At first, it was a single character: a winged woman with red hair. I didn't even know who she was, but the image stuck with me. From there, I began figuring out details about her origins and her world, but I only started writing for real in 2009. After over ten years of hard work, books of The Cyborg's Crusade are finally ready for release.